HW01007829

RUN, RUN RABBIT

CAMBRIC CREEK AFTER DARKVERSE

C.M. NASCOSTA

MEDUAS EDITORIALE

First edition published by Meduas Editoriale 2022

Interior Art by: BloodWrit

AUTHOR'S NOTE:

Author's Note:

Welcome to the Cambric Creek After Darkverse, where there's not as much sugar and a lot more spice. Our stories still take place in the community we already know and love, but these will not be the frothy, fun, cotton candy confections you're used to, and they will **not** all wrap up with a neat little HEA bow.

Content Advisories for Run, Run Rabbit include:

Primal play, chase play, public sex, knotting, non-monogamous relationship, shifted sex, inappropriate workplace romance, pregnancy termination, Is he an alphahole or just an asshole? and a decently toxic relationship.

THE PARTY

Chapter One

Lupercalia

High above the valley, the moon hung like a beacon, brightly lit and luminous. Despite the unseasonably warm weather, there wasn't a single cloud to hide its brilliance. As Vanessa sped along the rural highway, it seemed the moon was shining a spotlight down the road, lighting the way to the celebration like a bright, white runway.

She was already running late. Work always seemed to know when she had plans, creating a domino effect of late meetings and endless piles of paperwork, and once she'd arrived home, wardrobe indecision had set her back further. Now, she was attempting to make up for the lost time. The stretch of highway between Cambric

Creek and Starling Heights always seemed empty, no matter what time of day she traversed it, which wasn't often. Being the only car on the road often left her feeling discomfited, but she was grateful for the empty road then. There was no one to impede her progress, no one to slow her haste. No one to make her any later than she already was.

He would understand. Perhaps more than anyone else she knew, he would understand her tardiness and wouldn't care. *If he even notices.* After all, hadn't he been late just the previous month, the first time they'd spoken in several?

"You don't need to apologize," she'd smiled up once he'd finally appeared before the table that night in the over-priced restaurant he'd suggested, the waist-coated server ducking his head, pulling out the chair across from her for her tardy companion. The linen-covered table was already littered with the half-empty water and wineglass, the latter having already been refilled twice by the time he'd arrived, but it hadn't mattered.

"That's a relief," he'd grinned down, his skin still holding its sun-kissed glow, his perfect white teeth blinding her for a moment. He'd been on vacation a month prior to that night, somewhere in the Maldives with someone who wasn't her, and the knowledge had made her twist . . . but twisting had only ever made her fight harder. "Because I hadn't planned on it." His smile was cutting, but she had met it with a sharp-edged grin of her own. He was a wolf, a cocky, arrogant bastard of a wolf. But then again, so was she.

Vanessa reminded herself that he'd not apologized then, and she didn't need to apologize now. All she had to do was get there. The moving dot representing her car on the GPS's digital display showed how close she was to the hidden cul-de-sac where she needed to turn, following the circular road until she reached a private drive leading into the woods. Greenbridge Glen was the perfect backdrop for the nearly full moon. A tiny, sparsely populated hamlet, comprising a small resort and a smattering of private homes and not much else, nestled in the rolling hills of agriculture that stretched between the two towns. It was lush and green, the hills providing a perfect sea of shadows for the moon to cast her white light upon, guiding the way.

The house was a country estate, built at the turn of the previous century, replete with hundreds of winking leaded windows and deco archways, high on a hillside, surrounded by forested peaks and valleys. The Greenbridge Glen address was a tax shelter owned by several members of the Cambric Creek elite — a shifter who lived halfway around the world; the troll couple who had started the Food Gryphon chain; the heiress to the Deliquesce fortune, a ubiquitous home plumbing product marketed to minotaurs and centaurs; and several others, including the evening's host.

"You've got to be fucking kidding me . . ."

The vast estate was on a private drive, a perfect setting for that night's celebration . . . or at least it would be if the line at the valet wasn't ten cars deep. Vanessa sighed, tapping her lacquered nails against the edge of the steering wheel as she idled at the curb, watching as another sleek luxury sedan slid into the queue. *Eleven cars. Fuck it.* She didn't want to waste any more of the evening than she already had, taking her foot off the brake as a twelfth car took its place in the valet line. She would park down the road and hoof it up the hill, and she wouldn't be forced to waste any more of the party.

It had become one of her favorite celebrations of the year; ironic, as she'd only started celebrating it since she'd met him. *Lupercalia.* There was something primal about this night, a tumidity that would weight the air even before the smells of sweat and sex permeated the ceremony; a heavy sense of expectation that seemed to curl around her, lifting her hair and licking down her bare legs. *That's what happens when you get this many hard cocks in a room at once.*

The throng of merrymakers had spilled out onto the lawn, she saw as soon as she crested the steep incline, only needing to step through a bit of landscaping, her spiked heels sinking into the black mulch at the base of the manicured shrubbery. A scowling security guard appeared before her, the furrow between his eyebrows deepening as she produced her gilt-edged invitation with a flourish and a beatific smile. *It could have been worse,* she reminded herself, kicking away the remnants of the mulch that clung to the toe of her black patent leather shoe. *You could have wound up crawling through the bushes. You didn't need to climb a tree or hop a fence, so we'll call this a win.*

As usual, no expense had been spared. The champagne was already flowing liberally, waistcoated servers gliding through the crowd, crystal flutes, hot hors d'oeuvres, and identical black masks on hand for those who had not brought their own. Vanessa wondered, as she looked around at the sea of staid cocktail attire, snagging a champagne flute from a passing tray, how many of these gossiping guests would stay as perfectly coiffed as they were now; how many of them would fall prey to the hysteria of the festivities, loosening their hair and clothing alike when the wolves began to run. She paused, wrinkling her nose at the unexpected taste of the champagne, before straightening her black lace mask and entering the fray.

"Have you heard the news?"

Vanessa melted into one of the clusters of partygoers, sipping her champagne as if she had been there the whole time, raising an eyebrow at the woman on her left's excited utterance. "There's news? I must've missed it."

They were ecstatic to have a newcomer, this circle she'd joined, explaining and reexplaining the same gossip she had steeled herself to hear repeatedly through the night. The group around her tightened ranks, their circle closing, excited whispers piling together into an indistinct susurration until the dark-haired woman on her left leaned in again. "Jackson Hemming is running for mayor. You know what that means. Changes will be coming soon, mark my words, and they're all in our favor."

Vanessa had perfected an expression of artless innocence that served her well in the courtroom, and she employed it then. "Running for mayor where? In Bridgeton? I didn't think our election was for another two years! Just goes to show how much I pay attention,

I guess . . . I can't see a werewolf being elected, though, not with a human population of that size."

Several of the other guests huffed in exasperation at the foolishness of her comment. Of *course,* not Bridgeton — despite being the closest city, one of the largest in the state, where political aspiration might ripple beyond the well-insulated bubble of these privileged partygoers. She feigned ignorance as they corrected her misassumption, explaining the power dynamics in tiny, neighboring Cambric Creek. Multispecies. Werewolves and shifters started the town, didn't she know; *should* be running the town, and it was a relief that they would be again.

"I guess I've never been that interested in politics," she shrugged, setting her empty flute on the tray of a passing server before turning to move on. The champagne had a sweet effervescence, certainly a top-shelf choice and fine for a crowd this size, but it was hardly his favorite. *Correction:* ***some*** *expenses were spared.* "Jackson Hemming, he's the host tonight, right? I haven't met him." She turned away, unable to hold back her small, self-satisfied smile as the man to her right snorted in disgust at her ignorance.

She didn't wait to hear their corrections. Jackson *should* be there, she thought, moving on to the next group of people. He ought to be schmoozing and rubbing elbows, participating in the ancient rituals, leaving his judgment and the stick that lived up his ass at the door . . . but this wasn't his party, and that wasn't her business. One group of people turned into two, then three, on and on, the same tired gossip, identical masks, all blurring together until she was finally able to ascend the stone staircase, pushing through the crowd at the open, gilded doors.

The interior ballroom was similarly populated with broods of clucking hens and circling servers, but she knew it would not stay that way for long. Soon the altar space would be thick with incense and smoke. The music, which was currently so courtly and mild, would escalate slowly, gradually beginning to rise in intensity, nearly without notice. A drumbeat that would seem to thunder in her chest until her heart had absorbed its rhythm would keep the crowd in thrall as the wolves entered, as they ran, as the women in their path shrieked, skin striking skin, hands fitting against the curve of hips, cocks slipping between parted thighs like puzzle pieces slotting together. For now, though, the music was sedate, matching the elbow-rubbing that took place amongst this crowd of the well-heeled elite.

A slow scan of the room showed her where the altar space was set up and the doorways through which the wolves would enter. And there, along the far left wall, she saw him on a raised platform separated from the crowd by a gilded railing. The evening's host.

He was tall and impossibly broad with wide shoulders, heavy with muscle; a brick wall of a wolf. The definition of tall, dark, and handsome, at least she had always thought so, his square jaw and firm chin providing a striking profile, even with the black domino mask concealing the top portion of his face. The golden railing kept him separated from the rabble in an aloof bubble in the midst of what looked like a heated conversation with several other men.

"That's one of the Hemmings," hissed the woman who had sidled up to where she stood, following Vanessa's line of sight. Human from the smell of her, one of the seat fillers. Bursting with recently acquired knowledge and overeager to share, Vanessa thought, a suspicion the girl all but confirmed as she plowed on. "He's the host. And I think that might be one of his brothers behind him. And the short one is Hasty Harland. No, wait. That's not it. Harland Hast—"

"Harmond Hastings," Vanessa corrected, her eyes not leaving the bigger man's black mask. "Of Hastings–Durning Pharma."

The name didn't seem to ring a bell for the human girl, unsurprising considering she hadn't spent most of her ovulating life taking monthly heat suppressants bearing the Hastings–Durning name. Whoever had brought the girl was a name-dropper, but Vanessa gave her credit — she was clearly a quick study.

"But you're right . . . that *is* one of the Hemmings, and the other is one of the brothers. Probably the one running for mayor, he's all anyone is talking about."

It wasn't. Even with the mask, she could tell from across the room that it was Trapp standing beside Grayson, his megawatt smile hardened into a scowl, the only two expressions he seemed to possess, but this human didn't need to know that. *Better to cause confusion. That's how rumors get started.* Sure enough, the human woman's eyes widened behind her own mask, and Vanessa could almost see the gears turning in her head, the way her eyes darted around quickly, looking for someone with whom she might share this newly gleaned nugget.

Whatever conversation was taking place between the men, it didn't look like an especially friendly chat, and Vanessa rolled her eyes, turning away from the sight of the men and the human girl to insert herself into one of the many conversation clusters around the ballroom, hoping the ongoing gossip of the night wouldn't overshadow the actual ceremony.

"Have you heard the news?" The blonde who addressed her was the same one she'd stood behind outside the doors, eavesdropping as the woman complained to her companion over having to wear a mask, waiting until the last possible second to slip it over her head. Vanessa knew that beneath the black domino, she had wide green eyes and a permanently frozen expression, thanks to a few too many trips to the aesthetician, her eyebrows arched in a creaseless forehead. "The wolves are coming back into power!"

The masks worn by each attendee were identical, adding to the air of mystery and hedonism surrounding the events, an excellent touch added by the party planners. Even with the masks in place, Vanessa recognized the blonde woman as the owner of a small jewelry shop operated by the same family for several generations, the russet-haired man to her left the proprietor of a Main Street restaurant, and the satyr beside him from the local paper. A shifter couple with an important family name. A millennial bohemian who'd come wearing a nearly sheer stola, who had a loft in the city where she hosted gallery showings that doubled as prescription drug swap meets. *The Cambric Creek elite . . . and you.*

"I didn't realize they'd ever left power. Someone should have told Jack," she quipped lightly, earning a titter from several of the others, the satyr raising his champagne flute in agreement. "I can't believe so many people drove this far to discuss local politics," she went on, draining her glass. Every conversation from which she'd extricated herself had been of the exact same circular nature, of the last thing she wanted to talk about, and she'd only just arrived. "You *do* know that Cambric Creek is a flyspeck on the map in the grand scheme of things, right? From the way people are acting, you'd think it was the White House."

"It's a short jump from mayor to governor," the satyr cut in, his wide, pink mouth curved in a sly smile. "Especially these days, *especially* with a recognizable name. A name in a state with a heavy were population. Once you open that door, the sky's the limit. Governor. Attorney General, perhaps? Grayson does look so *good* on camera. Surgeon General for the trifecta . . . well, I suppose Trapp spoiled *that* part of the plan, but maybe the young one, pre-med aspirations from what I hear. Still, it's paving the road up for the next generation. If anyone actually thinks Jack has been resting on his laurels all these years, they've not been paying attention."

The others murmured their agreement, and she heated, his words leaving her with an odd sense of déjà vu and an uncomfortable twist in her stomach. She didn't belong with this well-heeled crowd any more than this satyr did, but she had discovered that she was able to completely disappear amongst them. Everyone in their whole little far-too-impressed-with-itself town whispered and speculated over the *werewolf orgies*, as she'd heard the parties called, but none of them would ever cop to having attended, even if they were permanent names on the guest list. No one knew who she was, why she was there, who she might have known — and more importantly, no one cared. The masks gave each guest the guise of invisibility . . . invisible to everyone but the smirking satyr. Tris Tatterswain saw everything, paid attention to *every*thing, and the weight of his all-seeing eyes chafed at her skin like a rasp of sandpaper.

"How do you keep getting in, Tris? Who invited you? This is a wolven holiday, are you aware?"

"Are you under the impression there weren't satyrs at the first celebration?" he shot back without hesitation. "Werewolves might have founded Rome, sweetie, but they didn't build an empire alone. And I'm fairly certain I was invited by the same person who invited you."

"Cambric Creek may be small, but the collective voice of our community shouldn't be discounted against a place like Bridgeton," burst in a churlish-voiced man on the other side of the group, clearly impatient with the current conversation taking place above his understanding.

Vanessa held the satyr's eye for an interminable moment as the conversation continued around them, Tris's shrewd smile never slipping.

"How dull," she interrupted again. "You should have met up and got this out of your systems before tonight. We're supposed to be celebrating the holiday, not having the same boring conversation every three feet." Gossip wasn't what this night was about, after all.

"I'm with you." The voice at her elbow belonged to a man she'd not noticed edging into the group, but once her nose caught his scent, she wondered how she'd been able to focus on anything else.

Her wolf rippled beneath her skin, too close to the full moon to *not* react to the smell of such virility, and as she turned, Vanessa worried she might rock off her heels. He towered over her, and his gleaming white smile was matched only by the sparkle in his bright blue eyes, beaming down at her. Honey-blonde hair, tanned skin . . . he looked as if he'd just stepped off the pages of a yachting advertisement, and deep inside, her wolf whimpered. *Down, girl.*

"Who gives a shit about politics on a night like this? That's not why we're here. At least," he lowered himself to brush his lips against her ear, "that's not why *I'm* here."

It was her wolf's fault, Vanessa reminded herself. The hedonism of the holiday, coupled with the fact that the full moon was less than two days away . . . it was embar-rassing to admit how desperate she was to be fucked, but it didn't change the reality of the situation. Every twenty-eight days, it was the same, a superficial heat brought on by her birth control. She'd be crawling out of her skin in the days leading up to the moon, hornier than should have been possible, and it usually didn't abate until after the moon had passed. Her wolf was just as frenzied, just as desperate to be fucked, just as whiny and needy as she was on two legs, and every month ended the same way — she'd not be happy until she'd taken a thick cock and an even thicker knot, her womb flooded, left a gasping, panting, cum-and-sweat-covered mess in the dirt — but at least it ended.

"That's definitely not why I'm here . . . but my dance card might be full," she laughed, almost able to hear the way his wolf growled at her own. Skating her nails down the front of his dress shirt, she felt the hard plane of his abdomen, the way his stomach muscles jumped beneath her hand. His cock was already swollen as she traced its shape, pressed to the front of his trousers, giving the tensity of the zipper a run for its money as he hardened. "I wonder how much he wants to come out to play?" she mused, giving him a final squeeze before releasing. "But I guess it depends . . ." He leaned down once more, nearly vibrating in eagerness, until she could dart her tongue out and lick the shell of his ear, her wolf begging to lick something else. "How fast are you?" She laughed again at his scowl, shrugging before depositing her second champagne flute on a passing tray. "The chase is half the fun, you know."

Vanessa felt eyes on her back as she moved on from the group, pushing through the crowd, stopping to grope several strangers and be groped in turn, one twisting her nipple until she cried out, stumbling, but she avoided turning to find the source of observation. She didn't need to turn and wouldn't give him the satisfaction. She knew what the weight of his eyes felt like, had felt them on her more times than she could count — across meeting rooms and courtrooms, through the glass wall that had separated them, across hotel lobbies and restaurant dining rooms, and the long, ridiculously extravagant backyard of his suburban home. She didn't need to turn; she knew he was watching, and that was enough.

She could pick out the event's seat-fillers with relative ease as she crossed the ballroom, for every party had them — giggling girls, humans mostly, with influencer-perfect hair and cleavage up to their chins. They came from all over, the plus ones of invited guests or pleading for entrance at the doors; all eager to say they'd actually gotten in, to go back to their universities and jobs, boasting to their friends that they'd fucked a werewolf. Their presence had irritated her in the beginning, but now she appreciated their role and the function they served. They'd all be cruising for the party's host upon entry, realizing in short order that their aspirations were too lofty and that beggars couldn't be choosers, giving the other attendees something to chase for the night. *We all have our roles to play.* After all, she hadn't been lying to the model-handsome stranger — the chase *was* the fun part. If he wanted to play, he needed to run.

Helping herself to another champagne flute, she moved forward, drawn in like a homing beacon by the man leaning against the far wall of the gilded ballroom, smirking at his leer as she approached. There was no hiding what they were, not on this night, nor what they'd all come for.

"I could smell your cunt from across the room," the stranger hissed against her hair as she leaned into him, not even bothering with hellos. "You're dripping already, and we haven't even gotten started. Do you want to take my knot, little girl?"

She didn't waste time with the pretense of wandering down this one's body, gripping the meat of his cock with her whole hand, squeezing until he grunted. He was a wolf, but she was as well, and there would be no seat-filler simpering from her, no wide eyes or innocent giggles.

"Just like that," the man groaned, shifting his pelvis until she could feel the flare of his cockhead, groaning when her hand squeezed again. "I want you to choke on it. Do you want to get down on your knees for me?"

She didn't, not really, but she didn't release him yet. "Is that how you want me? Helpless on my knees? Begging for it?"

"Begging to be fucked," he agreed, sliding a hand between her thighs, meeting no resistance. She hadn't bothered with lingerie, not that night. Besides, she spent too much on it for it to be ripped or discarded in the woods, gone forever. Far better to leave it at home, along with her inhibitions. His fingers were stubby and thick, and he groaned again when they pushed between her lips into her wetness. He was right – she was dripping.

"I want you to choke on my cock," he repeated, circling against her sloppily, "and then get down on your knees and beg for my knot. *That's* how I want you."

A pity for him, she thought, for she was unmoved. None of these wolves made her weak, none of them made her blood thrill with helplessness, and none of their knots would be enough to satisfy her. Vanessa could still feel eyes on her back though, and she shifted her body as the shorter man's hand withdrew, allowing her watcher to see as she squeezed the other man's cock. This wolf was right — she *was* dripping, had been since the moment she'd arrived, and her nose picked out *his* singular scent. Dripping and hungry and eager to be filled . . . but not just any knot would do.

"You'll have to catch me first," she smiled at the stranger, cock straining against her palm. His eyes narrowed when she released him, straightening the hem of her stola before turning away.

The atmosphere in the room had shifted, she realized, nearly without her notice, a sign that the ceremony was about to begin. The music's tempo had slowed, the string quartet winding down their shift before they were replaced with the drums, and suddenly there was a heat behind her, a hand that landed on her hip with a bruising force, hot breath stooping to reach her ear.

"I wasn't sure if you were coming tonight. Since you've been so *busy*."

The solid pressure of *his* arm pushed into the small of her back, leaving her unable to turn, and she flinched away from the deep voice at her neck. She heard the rancor there, unsurprising, since their schedules hadn't meshed all month, even though he'd tried. He'd tried to take her to dinner again, with no free evening materializing for either of them; had made a soft overture around the previous month's moon, but by then she was sitting in pre-trial hearings, with no ability to pull away. Vanessa had expected his acrimonious tone. She hadn't been as prepared, though, for the tinge of bitter hurt that laced his words.

"I have been. McClellan went to trial, but we wrapped up about a week ago." It had been closer to two weeks and she knew that he knew that, but the masks they wore were designed for hiding.

"Are you ready to run, rabbit? Found a cock you like the shape of yet? Picked which one you want to ride, which knot you want filling you? Or are you going to let us all take a turn?"

She grinned a sharp-edged smile, uncaring if the man behind her was unable to see it. Let him be hurt; let him be jealous. He would run that much faster.

"That doesn't matter, does it? If you're too slow, you don't get to play." *The chase was the fun part.* "Perfect time to walk back on bad decisions, under a moon like this. But I'm not going to let just anyone catch me. I'm hot shit, and whoever he is will have to work for it. If you want to win, you'll have to catch me first."

His laugh was low and rough, and her wolf reared, wanting to bite and fight with the owner of such a patronizing chuckle.

"If that's what you want. Run, rabbit. Let's see how fast you can move." When he released her, she nearly stumbled, looking up in time to see the back of his head as he strode past her, never pausing. His dark hair caught the golden-hued light from above, the crowd parting for him like the sea, swallowing him up until it closed in his wake, leaving her behind, alone in the ocean of masked strangers.

* * *

THE CHASE

CHAPTER TWO

6 YEARS EARLIER . . .

She had been trying to make Grayson Hemming chase her since the first day they'd met.

He was arrogant, imperious, and a world-class prick, and she disliked what her attraction to him said about her. Likely that she had daddy issues (she didn't), or that she was a shameless social climber (she wasn't), or that poor self-esteem made her tolerate toxic traits she'd not put up with if only she respected herself more (she quite liked herself, actually, and more importantly, she'd never been at a loss for male attention, which proved how absolutely without worth it was).

"Public defenders have the least transferable skills of any sector," he'd said bluntly during the second round of her interview process. "You've never had to work with a team. You've never had to undertake the discovery process or the intricacies of civil litigation. We don't just show up before the judge not knowing our client's name. Your resume is about as useful to me as a first-year law student's."

He'd been late that day. In court, they'd said, unavoidably detained, and the managing partner had opted to start without him. She'd seethed when he leaned back in his chair, crossing his arms in a way that suggested no further argument, and she'd wished he'd been unavoidably detained beneath a bus. His tight-lipped smile was smug, and there was something about the way he looked through her as if she were invisible, not worth his time, that made her fists ball at her sides. His dismissiveness caused something to misfire in her brain, a spark of defiance she'd been unable to tamp back.

"That's one way of looking at it," she'd gritted out. "A rather shortsighted viewpoint, if I'm being frank. Another perspective for you to consider — I've likely gone to trial more times than three of your most senior associates combined." She sucked in a breath before continuing, nostrils flaring. "I clerked for Judge Arnulf on the appellate circuit, and I've been in private practice for two years, starting at the bottom."

Another tight-lipped, supercilious smile. He leaned forward, steepling his fingers on the table, and Vanessa tried very hard not to notice the breadth of his shoulders as he did so. "Our clients have particular needs, Ms. Blevin," he began, the tone of his voice suggesting that he was speaking to a very small, particularly stupid child.

"And more importantly," she'd gone on forcefully when his mouth had opened to continue his interruption, "every client I defended was a shifter of some sort. I clerked for a wolf. I've been in a private practice that chiefly serves companies owned by other wolves. I'll do my job to the best of my ability for my client, regardless of who my client is, but human interests will never be my priority if they run contrary to my community's. I wonder how many of the other attorneys you have working here would be able to say the same with the track record to back it up. Trust me, Mr. Hemming, you're not going to need to give me directions to the elevator every time I need to leave my desk."

She had done her homework. Grayson Hemming wasn't the managing partner at this firm, but he was one of the most vocal. He had an in-house reputation as a ruthlessly efficient litigator and brought in the firm's largest clients, thanks partly to a prestigious family name. More interestingly, she'd thought, every pro bono case he'd taken in the last five years had centered specifically on werewolf advancement.

She'd seen his photo on the firm's website, but she'd not been prepared for the in-person anomaly. The huge man who'd breezed into the room nearly thirty minutes late loomed over her with a slight air of impatience, as if *he* hadn't been the one keeping them waiting. He seemed too young to be an equity partner, too big and muscular for a white-collar desk job, *far* too handsome to toil behind closed boardroom doors and in courtrooms all day. Tall and broad, he had glossy dark hair and piercing, nearly black eyes that held a silver gleam that gave away his less-than-human nature, not that she needed to *see* to know what he was.

His smell had overwhelmed her from the moment he'd entered the room, and she was able to smell *everything* about him, from the citrus and juniper notes of his high-end aftershave to the expensive leather of his shoes and every solid, meaty inch in between. More than that, though, she smelled his wolf. Pitch black, he smelled of towering pines and wet earth, sex and sweat, and something primal and vicious. Someone else had begun to speak, one of the other partners droning on about the firm's mission statement, but she couldn't smell any of *them*, as if no one else in the room existed other than him, trapping her in his cocky, penetrating gaze.

She didn't blink as he stared her down, and she didn't look away, and after a few moments, his smile split.

Gleaming white teeth with decidedly sharp canines, he had a dimple in his cheek, and she knew she was lost. His wolf growled at hers, and her legs dropped open beneath the table on their own accord. She wanted to pick a fight and then let him clear the desk and fuck her senseless right there, in front of everyone else in the room.

It should have been a sign, Vanessa thought looking back. She should have held her tongue the rest of the interview and then withdrawn her application, leaving to find a firm run by men who resembled her grandfather, not a sexy, imperious asshole. If she had known then how stupid he would make her, how she would make one bad decision after the next, all concerning him, she would have walked out and not looked back. But her wolf and her pride wouldn't let her walk away from the way he smelled, couldn't walk away from that sharp, cutting smile. She would stay, stay and prove him wrong. *At least until you come to your senses, you silly bitch. Walk away with your head held high. And until then, you show this smug asshole what you're made of until he's begging you to stay.*

* * *

Chapter Three

5 YEARS EARLIER . . .

"Do you have any plans for the holiday?"

She looked up in surprise, eyes wide, shocked by the overture of small talk and uncertain of what holiday she was meant to be celebrating. Vanessa watched as one of his dark, perfectly groomed eyebrows raised archly; every second she remained silent was a guarantee he'd go back to treating her like a piece of gum on the sidewalk.

"Lupercalia?"

"Oh!" she exclaimed with a small laugh, letting out the breath she'd been holding, feeling her cheeks heat.

"Oh, I-I guess not, not really. I used to make honey cakes with my mom when I was little, but I haven't done that in years."

"You don't celebrate then?"

His tone was nonchalant, but Vanessa sensed the loaded judgment in his words. She could tell he had already mentally reached his verdict and found her lacking. Lupercalia was an outdated holiday, her parents had always posited, and an adult one at that. As a child, her family had a special dinner and not much else. The first actual party she'd attended was at university, and it seemed little more than an excuse for the frat brothers to score with as many girls as they could in an evening, hardly an advertisement for werewolf pride and inclusivity.

"Well, so much for track records and defendants and all that bluster about community."

The smile he cast in her direction made every muscle in her body clench, and she tightened her grip on her phone to keep from throwing it in the direction of his perfect teeth. He was at the other end of the table, and she wondered if her almond-shaped manicure would be sharp enough to gouge out his eyes were she to vault herself like a ninja at him. *Next time get the stilettos. Harder to type but they have benefits.*

"But I suppose I have to give you credit—you weren't terrible today, rabbit."

***

She'd been there a year at that point. It should have been embarrassing, the way they'd made her start from the bottom, truly as little more than an office aide. The endless litany of tasks were things that would typically fall under the purview of a paralegal, some more befitting an unpaid intern. If there was grunt work to be done, Vanessa found it on her desk. She'd undertaken it without complaint, knowing the ladder only went up, and if she didn't make these bones on the bottom in front of these new firm owners, she would never be given access to the first rung.

Despite his vocal presence at her interview, she'd seen very little of the imperious, dark-haired partner. It seemed he was constantly in court, coming and going with a confident sneer or holed up in his executive suite office, with an endless team of researchers, junior associates, and paralegals working round-the-clock on his cases. Even though he'd made sure to knock her down a few pegs that very first day, Vanessa was certain Grayson Hemming was quite unaware of her existence.

Until the day that he was.

It had been a day like any other. She'd been coming out of a conference room, surrounded by a throng of people, carrying a stack of binder-clipped documents. He had been on the other side of the hallway, stopping abruptly in the middle of the corridor and nearly causing a pile-up of bodies in his wake. When his eyes locked on hers, she felt the air leave her lungs.

The smell of him was thick and impenetrable and clouded her brain, making the wide-open corridor seem like a tight box inhabited by no one but them. His head cocked slightly, and she felt the weight of his eyes slide down her body to the tips of her toes and up again, pinning her there like an insect under glass. She jolted when she'd realized she was the only one left still standing there gaping, that they were *both* standing there staring at each other like idiots, and had forced her feet to turn away from him, beelining to a bathroom to splash cold water in her face and get control over her breathing, trying not to notice the way her heartbeat seemed to thump in the space between her thighs.

Since that day, she'd felt his eyes on her constantly. She had never assisted on one of his cases and had never been given a reason to venture up to the executive floor, but wherever she was in the building, it seemed as if he found a reason to be there as well, however briefly.

Vanessa told herself that the haircut she'd splurged on was necessary for looking professional in the courtroom, even if it did make her dark hair seem fuller and flippier, and that the several new dresses she purchased were similarly to look polished and capable for her clients . . . and not that the body-skimming shapes and designer labels were for the benefit of her daily audience of one. The weight of his eyes would sink into her back, pressing down her spine, slipping over her legs like black satin. He was an asshole; a demanding, demeaning son of a bitch, but she had a very hard time pretending to herself that she didn't like the presence of his eyes finding her throughout the day, pressing to her like a kiss before he vanished.

The unfortunate side effect of being fully in his orbit of awareness was putting up with him. This was the first case of his upon which she'd been called to assist, which meant armloads of discovery documents dumped on her desk at regular intervals and a nonstop stream of highlighters from the supply closet, more late nights than she had ever worked in her life, and a continuous email chain from him demanding more, more, more. More work, more research, accomplished faster, with the subtle insinuation that if she couldn't keep up, she could see her way to the door. She had perfected the art of vomiting in a perfect stream into the toilet bowl and had invested in a giant case of breath strips that dissolved under her tongue, plausible deniability that she ever let the stress of the endless workload, going to federal court, or his barrage of insults, demands, and threats get to her.

Vanessa pursed her lips, huffing in offense at his words, hoping it disguised the giddiness she felt over the backhanded praise. The attraction she felt towards her arrogant, demanding boss was mutually returned; she was sure of it, but as of yet, nothing had happened, which was for the best, she reminded herself firmly. A year, she reminded herself, crossing her ankles demurely, feeling the slow drag of his eyes, meaning she should have been well over her crush. If a crush were all it was.

"He's a fuck boy," her coworker had laughed in the bathroom mirror, weeks earlier, leaning forward until her breath fogged the glass as she examined her mascara. "A total man whore. I've heard he has a new girlfriend every other week, but none of them stick. There has to be a reason."

Vanessa had rolled her eyes, snorting at the other woman's words. "The reason is that he's a fucking asshole," she answered succinctly. "That's not hard to figure out at all. A cocky, egotistical asshole. But he gets away with it because he's hot and he probably has a big dick. Besides, it's not fair to call someone that looks like *that* a boy, whether he fucks around or not."

Every bit of it was true. He was arrogant and sharp, onerous and demanding and a *mega* fucking asshole . . . and all of those things, combined with his flashing eyes and steely smiles, were apparently her Achilles' heel. It was humiliating to contemplate.

Her original desk had been far away from his office, but now she had been moved up several floors, and there were some afternoons Vanessa was positive she could smell him through the vents. The scent of his wolf seemed to send curling, black tendrils beneath her desk, licking up her legs and tickling her clit every time he was in the vicinity, and now that she had been given a chance to do work on one of the more prominent cases, it was ten times worse. She despaired over what might happen if she were ever called to sit behind him in court the week of the moon, with a shallow heat simmering in her veins. *Your honor, I'm not on his lap because of the case;*

it's just that I need to cock warm him until the change, or I'll go crazy. Surely the Multi-Species Disabilities Act covers that.

In retaliation, she preferred to fill her fantasies of him with scenarios of total control — *her* control. Every time a file was sent back to her because he wanted the same findings reannotated in a different color, she tried to imagine what he would look like stripped naked and bound in latex, strapped to one of those German torture porn tables, shiny black encasing his solid pectorals and heavy arms, whimpering while she edged his cock. When he made some cutting comment about her lack of beneficial experience, she wondered if he would still be as bossy and sharp with the spike of her heel pressing into the seam of his scrotum, which she imagined to be fat and full, for anyone with as much arrogance as he possessed would indeed be testing the strength of his fly every waking moment. Her favorite daydream involved watching his arrogant expression fade, aloofness replaced with panic when his airway constricted, suffocating slowly as she rode his perfectly chiseled face until he was purple and unconscious.

It was for the best that she'd not done something foolish to act on her attraction, and even better that he'd not either. She didn't need to be embroiled in some HR scandal that would follow her for the rest of her career. Her wolf didn't quite understand that, though, and she whined every month when the full moon neared, certain she could hear the pulsing in his balls and taste the heft of his cock on the air. All of her control fantasies fell away, and she could think of nothing other than the way he would dominate her in bed and fill her with his knot, the way he dominated opposing counsel in the courtroom — cooly confident, always in control. She'd always had a competency kink, and he set it on fire.

***

"I grew up in a human neighborhood, actually, so there wasn't much space for celebrating the holidays," she explained, unsure why she was doing so, knowing he would likely have something shitty to say in response. Instead, his brow softened, almost imperceptibly.

"Were you—"

"No," she answered quickly, already knowing he was going to ask if they had been eclipsed, werewolves hidden amongst humans, and she shook her head with her own tight smile. "I was raised to be proud of what I am. Proud . . . but quiet. You know how it is." She wasn't sure that he did, actually, but his eyes sparkled as she went on. "And besides, the few parties I went to at school left much to be desired."

"Well, I suppose you're going to need to get on the guest list for an *actual* celebration, in that case," he quipped lightly. "We need to get you caught up. You don't need to be quiet anymore, rabbit."

She wondered how quiet *he* was, if he moaned when he came or if he was stoic and silent, face turning red as his cock spurted, vocalizing nothing.

"Have you ever done cross in a federal hearing?"

His words snapped her out of filthy reverie, and she straightened. "No."

She braced for the insult, but all he did was nod, making a move to gather up his things. "Prelim is next week, you'll need to get caught up before then. If you have things on your calendar, move them. We may actually manage to turn you into a civil litigator yet."

"Five times," she exclaimed indignantly, throwing her hands up, the sight of that dimple appearing beside his perfect smile making her stomach swoop. "I've now gone to trial five times more than your three most senior litigators combined. I think we've dispensed with the 'yet' part of that. And why a rabbit?"

It was meant to be an insult, surely; an indictment of her work, appearance, and ability. She knew that was likely true, but the knowledge didn't detract from the giddy reality that Grayson Hemming had a pet name for her, even if it was meant to cut her down. She'd worked too hard all these months proving herself, had fought tooth and claw for a chance to reach that chair behind him at trial, and now that she was there, Vanessa decided she wasn't inclined to leave.

"Is that because I'm just so sweet and innocent looking in the courtroom? Men are easily fooled, you know. Did it ever occur to you that maybe that's *why* I've been to trial five times more than your best guys?"

His answering chuckle was a low rumble, a dark curl that seemed to slip its way between her thighs with ease, reverberating against the wetness it found. Her breath caught when he rose, moving with the same unhurried confidence he displayed in the courtroom. The pale color of his shirt was blinding next to his lightly tanned skin, the fabric taut, straining as he shrugged his jacket back on. Her lungs tightened, and she realized she was holding her breath as he crossed the room, moving in what she could only describe as a swagger. She wondered if he could smell how drenched she was already, the mere sight of his loosened tie enough to make her wolf writhe, raising her ass and presenting herself willingly.

She quaked when he lowered his nose into the dark tangle of her hair until his lips brushed the shell of her ear. She could smell him — the subtle expensiveness of his aftershave, the bourbon on his breath, the heat roiling off him. The wild, untamed smell of his wolf made hers whimper, and the thought of his jaws at her throat, his knot stretching her open and sealing her shut . . . Vanessa tightened her grip on the arm of her chair, sure she was about to slide off. *No way he doesn't smell that.*

"Because you smell like prey." His voice was a low hiss in her ear, a bolt of lightning straight to her cunt, and she could feel the self-satisfied smirk into which his lips curled, not pulling away. "Good enough to eat."

* * *

Chapter Four

4 YEARS EARLIER . . .

"So you don't actually know."

His words were impatient, the hand that jerked towards the door an aggravated dismissal as if she were nothing but one of the researchers. Her forehead wrinkled at his sharp tone, hands tightening around the file folder she carried as she shook her head.

"No, that's not what I said—"

"You said 'maybe,'" he interrupted, head lifting to pin her in place with his icy glare.

"'Maybe' isn't an answer. 'Yes, we have it, or 'no, we don't.' Do you see the difference? I need absolutes.

We're not going into court with a pocketful of 'maybes.' Do we have the signatures, or don't we?"

Her back stiffened, the desire to hit him with the folder making her arm shake. *Hit him and mess up that perfect fucking hair.*

"I said *maybe* Johanna hasn't emailed you yet, but they signed everything this morning. If only you'd let me finish my sentence before needing to bite my head off over nothing."

"*Maybe* you need to communicate your thoughts a bit more concisely."

"Or *maybe* we just need to fuck and get it out of our systems."

The words were out before she could swallow them down, her internal monologue bubbling to the surface and tumbling from her mouth with no way to snatch it back; the boldest, stupidest words she'd ever uttered.

She had just celebrated her second anniversary at the firm two months earlier, but the previous four months — having him right there, separated by a mere glass wall, in constant sight — had been nothing short of torturous.

"Unless you have a better solution for this shit mood you're in," she went on. *In for a penny, in for a pound.* "Because I'm all out of ideas, and I'm tired of being yelled at for giving you exactly what you're asking for."

***

It wasn't even his office. The senior associate Vanessa reported to had called the glass-walled office home, until the day she'd come in and the woman was gone, relocated, Grayson there in her place. She was vain enough to convince herself it was because of her and the proximity to her desk, at least at first, but by the end of the workday, she'd heard that he'd informed the managing partner that he would walk out that day and not come back if he had to spend one more afternoon working under harsh fluorescent lights. He'd been hastily relocated to the makeshift office, and the entire upper suite was now scheduled for a renovation. By the end of the day, the glass fishbowl-like walls had been fitted with black curtains that were kept closed over the following weeks. Closed, except for the wall that faced her desk.

The track lights were almost always off, even when he had the curtain facing her open, and the sight of him there in the darkened room — suit jacket draped over the chair in the corner, shirt sleeves rolled up, his mouth and hands in perpetual motion as he took phone call after phone call — was driving her crazy. She'd watched him on more than one occasion with his head tipped back, eyes closed, fingers circling over his right temple. She imagined herself slipping into the cube-like room, closing the curtains securely and locking the door before dropping to her knees in the darkness before him, drawing down the zipper at the front of his pants, and swallowing his cock whole.

He had been snappish with her for the last several weeks, in a way that felt oddly personal, even though his words were icily professional. He still acted like an entitled asshole in general, looking down his nose at everyone, but Vanessa didn't know what she had done to have been singled out in such a way, and she was tired of his unexplained ire.

. . . And now she had just offered to fuck him, had made the suggestion here, at work, in his office, in the middle of the day, with no martini lunch in sight on which she could blame it.

Grayson cocked his head, considering her words as if she had just offered a solution to a problem they were running into with the case and not something horrifically inappropriate over which she might be fired. He rolled his pen between his thumb and forefinger — a Montblanc in black ink, the only ones he would use.

She had watched a month earlier when he had risen from his desk, carrying the brand-new, unopened box of office supply store pens that had been left for him, tipping it into the trash. When she'd tapped on the glass a short while later, struggling to find the opening in the curtains and flailing like a ghost for several seconds as he snickered, she'd made a point of looking into the waste basket.

"You're too good for the office pens?" she'd observed as he looked over the paperwork she'd placed on the desk, crossing her arms, waiting for a sputtering denial.

"Yes."

He didn't bother denying it, and she couldn't help grinning at his brazen arrogance. *Such a prick. Such an unmitigated asshole. So entirely fuckable.*

"So are you, rabbit," he went on, glancing up at her beneath a long fringe of lashes and his thick, dark brows.

"How do you know that?" she shot back. "You've never asked me a single question. You don't know where I come from or what kind of family I have. Maybe I grew up in the system or came from a pack. You don't know anything about me."

Her words had no effect on him, never looking up from his own signature as the stupidly expensive pen flowed across the paper.

"Aside from the fact that you already mentioned your childhood in a human neighborhood, none of that matters. People remake themselves all the time. You're never better or worse than the person you are each day. You wouldn't be sitting in this room if you weren't. And don't presume to tell me what I know."

Her stomach had flip-flopped, her insides seeming to liquefy when he went on seriously, looking up, at last, trapping her in the intensity of his bittersweet chocolate gaze.

"*You* are your most valuable asset. Your time is your most valuable commodity. Your name, whatever you want to call yourself, is the outward label of all you are. So don't denigrate it with garbage."

When he'd handed her back the folder of paperwork, one of his overpriced pens had been inside, and she'd floated out of the glass office with a small smile and her heart thumping, putting a newly-acquired dildo to work as soon as she got home that night, clenching around its knot and thinking of him, nearly sobbing as she came.

***

And now you've offered to fuck him for real.

"It's interesting to me," he mused, his voice never losing its disaffected tone, "that you always seem to be under the impression that you're a step ahead, Ms. Blevin, when the reality is you're three steps behind."

She sucked in a shaky breath, hating him. *You have this place on your resume now. You should start looking for something else.* The thought of seeing him again after this was too mortifying to contemplate, and she was furious with herself for her ill-spoken words, the desire that had spurned them, and her crush on this self-aggrandizing dick.

"I want to see the lab findings again. Leave the deposition. You have the audacity to come stomping in here and say that to me as if not only is it just occurring to you, but that you're also laboring under the mistaken impression that I hadn't already concluded that."

Her mouth dropped open, and fire ripped through her veins, heating her core until her legs could barely hold her, but the look he leveled on her was nothing short of disdainful.

"Lab findings. We go to trial in a week, rabbit. I need you upright for that." He leaned forward, and almost as if she were being pulled on a string, she did as well. "And if I fuck you now," he went on in a low scrape, a vibration she felt between her thighs, "you won't be. So until then, let's start having faster conversations."

There was a note beneath her door when she finally arrived home that night, building management notifying her that her mailbox in the apartment lobby was full to bursting. She kept a PO box for that very reason, stomping down the hallway to the elevator, mumbling to herself about Grayson Hemming until she reached the lobby. Her panties were drenched. She was furious with herself, furious with him, and she still didn't know what she had done to earn his ire over the past several weeks.

The small mailbox was packed so tightly with junk mail that she needed to yank it out at an angle, several store flyers fluttering to the floor. It was primarily circulars and credit card applications, all garbage she had no use for, but the presence of a gilt-edge caught her eye as she walked back to the elevator, her stomach flip-flopping in trepidation the entire ride up to her apartment. *Your company is cordially requested . . . Lupercalia . . . ancient celebration . . . brotherhood of the wolf.*

There was no one else she knew who would have celebrated a werewolf holiday in such lavish fashion, no one else who'd ever asked her about her holiday plans. *He invited you to a party for a holiday that's literally about fucking, and you never even opened the godsdamned invitation.*

Vanessa dropped into a chair, shoulders shaking in manic laughter. He'd at least had the grace and professionalism to attempt fuck her outside of the workplace first and had even sent her a fancy invitation in which to do so. *And you propositioned him right there in his office.* She understood why he'd been so snappish with her and found she could even forgive him for the churlish, childish behavior. He'd been thinking about fucking her, *wanted* to fuck her, and she wondered how long he'd been doing so. One thing was certain, she decided — she quite liked having Grayson Hemming chase her, and she wasn't inclined to let him stop.

* * *

Chapter Five

3 YEARS EARLIER . . .

The elevator car, like everything else in the historic building in which the posh, old-money hotel was housed, was ornately designed. Art Deco scrollwork graced the grating, with Doric columns embossed on the gilded walls. The back wall was papered in a lush, dark red, giving the tight space the air of a luxury bordello, appropriate, considering her company.

She'd recently celebrated her thirty-second birthday, spending the evening the same way she'd celebrated her official third anniversary at the firm — slumped over her desk until late in the evening, sifting through paperwork, wondering if the pretty twenty-something shifter who'd recently started in reception was entertaining one of the partners that night. *A specific partner.* She'd mumbled to herself as she left that it wasn't worth it, that she ought to have chosen a career path that offered a healthy work-life balance, and that it wasn't too late to change.

Then again, she reminded herself, those late nights meant she got to come along to meetings like this, held in swanky midtown hotels, their clients not deigning to leave their hotel room for something as inconsequential as a meeting with their legal team. They were merely the help, invisible employees to people like this, and even though she knew she was included in that equation, the fact that Grayson was as well made her giddy.

They had reached the end of their three-year tango, it seemed. She'd put a sledgehammer through the wall of careful restraint that had kept them at a respectable distance, kept her fantasies merely that — fantasies, enjoyed privately and with a succession of men who weren't him, whose names she didn't remember, none of whom had fucked her as hard as she was sure he would.

The trial had been all-encompassing, the biggest she'd assisted on, for one of the firm's most important clients, and there hadn't been a spare minute of any day to dwell on that night in his office, but now the trial was over, and the full moon was just a few days away. The smell of him was driving her mad, and the thought of his cock, the heft and taste of it, was the only thing on her mind.

She had been unable to tear her eyes away from the shape of it the previous afternoon as he'd reclined in his leather office chair, using his heel to swivel in lazy half-circles as he took a seemingly endless call. She'd sat frozen, unable to breathe, unable to blink, captivated by the sight of his open legs and the bulge pressed against his thick thigh, outlined perfectly in the slate grey trousers. Her mouth had been slack, her work forgotten, and she'd leaned forward a bit in her chair, the outline of his fat cock the only thing that existed, until she'd realized he'd ceased his movements. He'd watched her watching him, never ending his phone call, but under the weight of her eyes, she had witnessed the shape of him thicken and expand, hardening for her audience until it had been a solid bar of flesh, straining against the fine grey wool, a promise of what he might do to her.

"What are your plans for the rest of the day?"

His deep voice shook her from her ruminations, unsure of how she was meant to answer, knowing he would likely pile her desk with paperwork. The colleague that had been in the car with them had just exited on the twelfth floor, where the sky bridge to the parking garage was located, but she had planned on stopping at the little café at the street level, just outside the hotel doors, treating herself to an overly sweet coffee drink before trudging back to their office.

What she *wanted* to do was go home; go home and get away from him and his laconic voice and maddening smell, force herself to go out with her friends and find a dark-eyed, deep-voiced stranger to fuck, if only to take the edge off before the moon that weekend, a futile effort, but one she employed every month.

"I was going to stop and get a coffee before heading back. Are-are we already starting this case? Did you need me to pull anything up for you when I get back?"

Grayson's eyes remained fixed on the doors, his sculpted jaw and sharp cheekbone in perfect profile against the red wallpapered backdrop, his expression impassive, ignoring her question.

He put in an enormous amount of effort. That, she was unable to deny. Unlike a large swath of the nameless, faceless succession of casual bed partners she'd entertained, his comportment was immaculate. Never a hair out of place, groomed within an inch of his life. Even on the days when the light in his office stayed off and his head tipped back, his knuckles white from the force with which he gripped the arms of his chair, not moving to the degree that she couldn't tell from her place on the other side of the glass if he was even breathing, he looked impeccable. His nails were blunt and buffed, the result of a regular manicure; whoever did his eyebrows was, she was forced to admit, better than her own girl, and his smooth, supple skin spoke to the likelihood that he probably used a moisturizer that cost more than her monthly car note. He was gym-hardened and well-tailored, and while he'd certainly hit the genetic lottery, that he put in effort couldn't be discounted. She swallowed, waiting for his answer, annoyed that the *effort* was one more thing she liked about him.

"I'm getting a room." His voice was casual, as though he were musing over what to order for lunch or some other trivial thing equally as unimportant. "Have you stayed here before? The concierge can get your coffee if you want the place outside."

The air in the elevator had vanished, her lungs seizing. Vanessa shook her head silently. His wide mouth quirked up in the ghost of a smile, but his eyes never left the gilded door of the car. She was unable to answer. Her mouth had gone dry, and her throat refused to work, suddenly feeling as though she were standing at the edge of a great precipice, one of her own making, and it was time to either leave or leap.

"I suppose this is the part when you have choices to make, rabbit," he murmured, echoing her thoughts. "You can get your coffee, and I'll see you on Tuesday, after the full moon. Or," he mused, his hand reaching out, a long finger slowly depressing the button for the lobby, "you can come upstairs with me, and we can get this over with. I'll even pretend you thought of it first."

He turned to face her at last, smile splitting as she stiffened in outrage. *Get this over with.* It was hardly an indictment of mutual desire. He was an unimaginable asshole, the worst sort of person, and she would rather spend the next two days before the turn chewing glass than spend another minute in his infuriating company. His eyes sparkled like obsidian as his smile stretched, and she wanted to claw the dimple off his face.

"'Let's get this over with,'" she repeated with a sneer, fists clenching as she turned to face him. "Well, how can a girl resist a romantic proposition like that? I think that's what my dentist told me before he performed a root canal. At least there I got a free packet of floss."

"Is that what you need?" He seemed to fill the whole car in a way he hadn't done only seconds earlier, and her heart tripped up her throat. He'd turned as well, stepping into her space, overwhelming her with his size until she began to shake like a leaf and her knees nearly buckled. "Romance?"

She ought to leave, she knew. She ought to spring out of this car second the door opened again and leave him standing there. Instead, Vanessa found herself melting against him when a giant hand dropped to her hip, pulling her flush to the long line of his body. She wasn't prepared to be kissed. She hadn't expected it from him, and kissing him hadn't been a part of her numerous fantasies, but when he bent to meet her mouth, their lips slotting together like a hand-carved puzzle, she knew she wouldn't think about anything else ever again.

His teeth tugged at her lips, tongue demanding entrance, as bossy as he ever was, and her wolf was too eager to give in. With every pass of his mouth, he sucked her lip between his own with a slight nip of his teeth, and each time, the gentle pressure made her clit throb. She ran her tongue over the blunt edge of his teeth until she reached the point of his canines, imagining how they would drag against her skin, nipping at her inner thighs, biting her neck as he knotted her.

He was arrogant and haughty, and she still wanted to step on his balls, but she also wanted the rest of it. Her wolf wanted his, and she wondered if their bodies would fit together as neatly as their mouths did. Her nails scraped over his erection, and he growled against her, teeth catching her lower lip one last time before he pulled away slowly.

"Tell me what it is you want, rabbit. Let me give it to you."

This *was* what she wanted, she realized. Grayson Hemming chasing her. His knot cooling the fire in her blood would merely be a bonus.

"Remind me again what you're offering?"

His low laugh vibrated against her, his eyes taking on the silver gleam that she knew was reflected in her own. The smell of him was making her crazy, and she wondered if the scent of her was what had made his cock so hard.

"Let's see . . . you can follow me upstairs and spend the next few days in a very luxurious hotel room, letting me fuck you until you can't walk." He shifted, letting her feel the press of his erection. "I can smell how needy and desperate your cunt is, how much you *want* me to fuck you. Do you think I can't? Do you think I can't taste how wet you are for me every month? How crazy the smell of your cunt makes me?" She pressed into him, whimpering when he rolled his hips slightly, letting her feel the shape of him rocking into her. "So let's stop playing games, Ms. Blevin, and let me give you what you want. I think that's a bit more generous than floss."

Her chest heaved, unable to deny a single word.

"This *is* what you want, correct? I believe this was *your* idea?" Her cheeks heated, joining the flush moving up her body at the thought of what he promised. '"We should fuck and get it out of our systems,' right? Is that what you want, rabbit? Are you still going to give me that pissy little look when you're bouncing on my knot? Or are you going to shut up for once and let me give that pretty pussy what she needs?"

Every nerve in her body felt electrified, every muscle pulled taut. She wanted everything he was offering — his teeth, his knot, his cock buried balls-deep within her. When he straightened up, stepping away, she whimpered.

"Or, you can push that basement button, and I'll see you next Tuesday. Either way, whatever happens — it doesn't matter. Because we're both professionals. No matter your choice, it won't affect anything when we return to the office."

The whole world seemed to sway as the elevator bounced, and she realized she was the only one who could make this decision. *Leap or leave.* If she left, it would be done, she knew without question. He would never proposition her again, would never mention it again, and they would go back to the status quo on

Tuesday, just as he'd outlined. She wasn't sure why she believed him. Everyone knew that getting involved with a coworker was the dumbest thing one could do in the workplace while getting involved with a superior — practically career suicide.

Even so, he'd never given her any reason for doubt before. He was sharp and demanding, but he was that way with everyone, looked his nose down on everyone . . . but he hadn't looked through her like she was invisible since that very first day. The only loser in the equation would be her, but she trusted him to not let that happen. And besides, she thought, unable to deny it to herself — she liked having Grayson Hemming chase her, and if she left now, he would never do so again. The elevator dinged, the doors opening slowly as he gave her a sharp-edged grin. He didn't move, letting her make her decision.

She never turned around, but Vanessa was sure she could feel the smugness of his smile radiating at her back as she stepped through the doors, letting him follow her to the lobby.

***

"Are you going to come on my mouth, rabbit? I want you to rub that perfect pussy on my tongue until I can't breathe. I want to hear you moan for me."

Every word sent a ripple of fire through her; every filthy, reverent word he'd uttered all weekend, a non-stop commentary on how beautiful she was, how incredible she smelled, how hot she made him, how good she felt, and what he was going to do to her next. Vanessa realized she was possibly the only person at the firm who knew this side of him existed, and the knowledge itself was nearly as exhilarating as his words. She keened when his huge hands gripped her ass, encouraging her to ride his mouth the same way she'd ridden his cock the night before.

"You're such a fucking *asshole,*" she wheezed above him, jolting every time he sucked her clit, scoring his scalp with her nails. She hated that he was *good* at this too; sucking, kissing, and licking with steady pressure until her control broke. She wondered if he knew she had fantasized about doing precisely that, riding his face until he was unconscious.

It had been so much like her fantasies — sinking her fingers into his dark hair and gripping tightly as her hips rolled, feeling the slide of his tongue and the bump of his nose — that when she came above him, it almost felt like a dream. She flooded against his mouth as he groaned, squeezing her ass and drinking her up. His face had been drenched when she'd finally fallen to the pillow beside him, and she was disappointed to realize she'd not even checked to see if he'd blacked out at any point. *Next time. We ride him until he's purple next time.*

What had begun as "fuck once and get it out of our systems" in that posh hotel room had necessitated him being *in* her system, and once he was there, her desire for him spread like an infection.

He couldn't get enough of the way she smelled, he'd said. Accused her of short-circuiting something in his brain, driving him to distraction, doing it on purpose! And she'd felt vindicated for her own reaction to his heavy, black scent all those months. Vanessa congratulated herself for having never gone up to the executive suite to crawl beneath his desk and press her nose to his balls, for if her desk had been any closer to his office, she was certain Grayson would have not had the same restraint. The instant the hotel door had closed behind them, his mouth had lowered, sucking at her throat, digging his fingers into her thighs as he backed her up against the bed.

"You smell so fucking good. I'm going to devour you, rabbit."

Prey. That was what he'd said, that she smelled like prey, something to be chased. Prey he was ready to devour. Vanessa sucked in a lungful of him, gripping a fistful of his shirt. She *liked* being chased, enjoyed having him on her tail . . . but the smell of his wolf and the promise of his cock were too great. It was time to be caught, but that didn't mean she would present herself to him like a good little bitch. She'd scraped her nails over his erection again, pressing her palm to the shape of him, squeezing his cock.

"Don't forget I'm a wolf too, Mr. Hemming. Are you going to let me put my teeth on your cock? Scratch your skin? Can I scrape you raw?" She squeezed him again, her blood thrilling when he yanked open his belt. She expected him to open his pants, to pull his cock out for her . . . instead, he gripped her wrist, pulling her hand in to grip the solid shaft of his erection.

"Do you see what you do to me? How hard just the smell of you makes me?" His fingers directed hers to cup the meat of his scrotum, a growl vibrating his chest when her nails dragged over his balls. "You can do whatever you want to me, rabbit. But I'm going to taste that pussy first."

He'd kissed her clit the same way he kissed her lips, with gentle pressure and suction, the drag of his teeth and the swipe of his tongue, until her thighs had trembled, her muscles pulled taut as bowstrings. Groaning when she came, he'd pressed nose and mouth to her as she shook, as if she were the finest vintage and he couldn't slake his thirst.

She wasn't sure why she was surprised that Grayson Hemming had the biggest cock she'd ever ridden, because fucking of course he did. *Stupid, arrogant, big-dicked asshole.* Undressing him for the first time had been like unveiling a work of art, her mouth following the line of dark hair his parted shirt buttons revealed, down his chest and stomach until her lips met his open belt buckle, and the solid, steel-like bar of flesh that had bounced out of his pants had nearly given her fucking black eye. Impossibly thick and veined, his foreskin did nothing to hide the shape of his fat cockhead, retracted just enough to show a circle of shiny-pink glans that attracted her tongue like a blinking light.

The first press of him within her made her head drop back, and that was all he did for several minutes — press his head in, breaching her continually until she was writhing, desperate for more. Her breath caught when he pushed in fully, stretching her wide, slowly, burying himself balls-deep within her while he could, before his knot swelled. She thought it didn't seem fair for him to have so much. To be handsome *and* successful was already bad enough; to have checks in the first two columns *and* possess the sort of penis songs were written about seemed practically unethical. *It's why he has such a bad personality, to balance out the huge dick.*

"You feel so good," he'd groaned into her hair. "Like you were made for my cock."

She hated admitting he was right. She hated *him*, hated his stupid smug smile and wretched dimple and perfect fucking hair, hated the sound he made as her nails dragged down his chest, *hated* that his cock felt so good. He was right — it was as if he'd been made for her. His thick shaft rubbed against every inch of her, reaching every hidden nook and cranny, spots within her she didn't even know existed. Vanessa thought of full moons past and the lackluster partners with whom she had often shared the lead-up, desperate to satisfy the heat in her blood with anyone available. None of them had felt this good, and none had fucked her half so well. Every thrust was hard and deep, their bodies pressed together in a way that kept his pelvic bone moving against her clit, giving her constant stimulation, and she might have been ashamed of the noises she was making — high desperate gasps, begging and pleading him fill her up and give her his knot — if she wasn't going cross-eyed from the pleasure.

"Just like that, fucking stars . . ." Her hands were tight in his hair, damp with perspiration as he rutted into her. Vanessa felt as though she might shake apart, babbling against his shoulder, each rock of his hips twisting the band of tension behind her navel tighter. "You feel so *fucking* good. Give it to me just like that. I hate you so much . . . I want you to rearrange my fucking *guts* with your big cock. I want your knot, please, please give it to me . . ."

She felt the moment he began to move with urgency, the drag against her g-spot and the pressure against her clit, his hips snapping, and she was gone. Vanessa sucked in a shuddering breath, her climax hitting her like a solid punch to the gut. Radiating up her spine and shaking her limbs, all she could do was cling to him.

She'd grown up well removed from anything resembling pack society. She'd never been told as a child that she should want to marry a big, strong alpha, and she didn't even believe in bullshit like bonding and scent mates, but as his teeth snapped at her throat, it was hard to believe that they *weren't* meant for each other at that moment. All she wanted was for him to lock his teeth on her neck and seal her with his knot. She could feel it, bumping the mouth of her opening, promising a delicious pain-streaked pleasure . . . but instead, he led her hands to the pulsing bulb of flesh at the base of his cock.

"Squeeze me," he rasped against her neck. "Milk my knot, babydoll. I'm going to fill you up, rabbit. I'm going to fill you till you're dripping."

It wasn't how she wanted to squeeze him, but as he continued to piston against her sharply, it was clear he had no intention of knotting her just then. His orgasm moved in a ripple up his back, his hips moving with pulse after pulse into her, and if she's been knotted tight, Vanessa was confident the pressure of each one would have tipped her over the edge once more.

***

She had her first taste of five hundred dollar champagne, Billecart-Salmon Le Clos Saint-Hilaire, his preferred bubbly, and she'd been unable to suppress her giggles when the bottle was uncorked at their table. He was a ridiculous snob, but Vanessa thought she could get used to this treatment.

"Why should we denigrate ourselves with garbage?" she tittered, raising her glass to clink against his, worried she would leave a slick stain on her seat when he returned her glinting smile, her pussy throbbing.

"Exactly."

He seemed entirely at home with the white glove service, used to being waited on. *You are from completely different worlds.* A smaller, more scathing voice in her head piped up, competing with her standard inner monologue. *Why does that matter? He's only interested in fucking you, and now that he has, things will return to normal just like he said.* Vanessa pinched her leg to break the voice, shaking it away. Instead, she listened with a raised eyebrow as he ordered, eliminating everything which may have contained an ounce of flavor from his meal, she thought.

"I wouldn't have pegged you for a picky eater."

He chuckled, sipping from his glass of expensive champagne. "I have a lot of dietary restrictions. It has nothing to do with being picky."

"Watching your girlish figure?"

The smile he gave her then was particularly sharp, his canines longer than they had been just a few days prior. "Migraine control, actually. Not that it helps much. I should bite the bullet and eat all the delicious aged cheeses."

She thought that his exit from his own office and temporary relocation to the fishbowl suddenly made an enormous amount of sense, considering the time he spent with the lights off in his office. She frowned. "Isn't there anything you can take?"

"Pharmaceuticals are formulated for humans, Ms. Blevin. Not for us. Hastings–Durning is one of our biggest clients for a reason. It doesn't matter what I take because it burns off with the turn. Same as if you were to take over-the-counter pain meds for a headache the week of the full moon. It's not designed for our systems."

His next question brought her up short. "Why didn't you move into the DA's office? You would have done well there."

Okay then, obviously, we're done talking about him. Vanessa hadn't expected him to bring up anything pertaining to work. She'd assumed he might avoid the reality of how they knew each other and their connection, but what else were they to talk about?

"I'm not so sure about that. The burnout rate is high for public defenders, and it's not much better for ADAs. I thought about moving into the prosecutor's office, plenty of folks retiring from that job, but it felt too much like switching teams. The laws always favor humans, and I liked being able to do my part to defend those who wouldn't have had advocacy otherwise. But I also didn't want to have a nervous breakdown before I was thirty-five, so here I am. As worthless as a first-year law student."

His dimple made an appearance, and her cheeks flushed. "I disagree. You would've done well in the DA's office. You're very passionate, extremely talented. The judges like you, and juries want to like you. I have no doubt you would've had a fine career there. Of course, private practice is *far* more lucrative. You're just taking up space under our roof now, but at least you're not still covered in grime from county."

She gasped in offense, pressing her thighs together as he laughed, like a spill of dark chocolate, raising her glass to clink against his, earning another of those glinting smiles. "What about you?" she huffed. "What made you go into law?"

"I've always been exceptionally good at arguing with people," he grinned. "Parlaying that into a career seemed obvious."

"Were you one of those debate team douchebags?"

"Oh, team captain," he agreed with a laugh, eyes sparkling. "Obviously. Pretty sure I hit the douchebag trifecta, actually." He proceeded to count off on his fingers. "Debate team. Lacrosse *and* I pledged Alpha Sigma Lupe."

Vanessa leaned over the table, giving him her best wolf-like smile. "Ohhhh, you were one of *those* douchebags. I pledged Delta Delta Lupe. We used to party with the Alpha Lu guys on campus."

He leaned forward on his forearms, shifting in a way that made her foot bump his shin. "Ahh, that tells me everything I need to know. Everyone knows what Delta Lu girls are like. If we had been at school at the same time, I would've had you on the front lawn of the house." Beneath the table, he caught her foot, his thumb pushing into her arch in a way that made her gasp. She knew the hands and feet were supposed to be conduits to the rest of the body, and as he caressed her skin lightly, she was sure he was hitting the pulse point that had a direct line between her thighs.

"I wouldn't be so confident about that, Mr. Hemming. I was hot shit in school."

"Still are," Grayson said simply, dropping her foot to rest on the bulge at the front of his pants. "I have no doubt you would've made me work for it. But I still would have had you."

Vanessa let her smile stretch, twinkling at him as her toes curled, caressing the shape of his erection. "You would have had to catch me first."

Another bottle of champagne was ordered for the room, and her head spun at the excess.

"You have the prettiest tits I've ever seen," he'd breathed against her sternum, his tongue following a sticky trail of champagne between her breasts, sucking her nipples until they were puffy and swollen, and she'd held onto his hair as he kissed his way down her body, shouldering open her legs, mouth delving once more between her thighs.

When she'd lain wheezing under him a short while later, on knees and elbows with his arms braced around her, his chest flush to her back and his teeth at her shoulder, gasping as his cock thumped into her solidly, she didn't believe that they could simply go back to the way things were on Tuesday.

He'd sucked five-hundred-dollar champagne off her nipples, and she had sucked his cock, squeezing his knot to increase his pleasure, feeling him pulse against her lips when he filled her mouth in an endless ejaculation and had listened to the percussion of his heartbeat, pressed against his chest as she drifted to sleep. After she had ridden his face the following morning, after sleeping in his arms, she was positive they could not go backward. But all through the weekend, time rarely spent outside of the room as he sated the fire in her blood and she drained his balls dry, he never knotted her, refusing to do so.

"I think . . . that's something we'll both regret, baby. Too soon. And I don't do that with new partners. I'm sorry, rabbit. I don't want to hurt you, and I don't know how much you can take. You're already so tight."

They couldn't go back, she knew when he kissed her, just before they left the room for the final time, his hand already on the doorknob. She thought his lips had quirked into a small, soft smile as he pulled away, and the bubble of warmth she'd felt had carried her all the way down to the lobby . . . Where he put her into the rideshare he'd already ordered, sending her off to face the full moon alone. When she walked into the office two days later, it had been business as usual.

"I want to see every reference to this specific test in their case files; let's go back at least three years. In blue. No — in green."

There hadn't been anything in his voice that would have betrayed what they'd done, no softening in his expression as he continued to bark orders, and she realized he had meant what he'd said. No matter how she chose, it wouldn't affect anything when they returned to the office, and so it hadn't. Vanessa reminded herself she ought to be glad. This was her career, and her career was worth more than five-hundred-dollar champagne and the deeply sexy way he smelled fresh out of the shower. She'd made the mistake of letting him catch her, and now that she'd been caught, he was done chasing.

He said it wouldn't matter, and she decided to follow his example. If it didn't have something to do with a case or client, she put it out of her mind, focusing on nothing but work in the following weeks, shifting the angle of her desk just enough that the inhabitant of the darkened, glass-walled office was out of her peripheral view. It didn't matter, and she didn't need to let it matter.

* * *

Chapter Six

When the full moon approached again, she took several moon days, something she'd not done since university. She didn't want to be there in the office, smelling him, twisting in her seat, writhing under the weight of his gaze, and letting him smell how needy he made her. Instead, she took herself out of the equation.

The man with whom she spent two of her sick days was someone she had hooked up with before, someone she'd met in a club frequented by shifters. He was well built and good looking, and he satisfied the ache in her blood well enough that she could function, and in another lifetime, she would've been attracted to him. Now though, the scent of him hit her nose wrong, and the shape of his body against hers felt as though they were from two different puzzles with roughly complementary edges; good enough, but not a perfect fit.

The day after the moon, she snuggled under a quilt on her sofa, warming her hands with an oversized mug of tea, and logged in to work for the first time since she'd left the office before lunch several days earlier. He had sent her a schedule tap the last morning she'd been in and an email with a blank subject line.

Do you have anything on your calendar this week?

It was innocuous and inoffensive and could have absolutely been about work, which was the point. *Plausible deniability.* The only thing on the calendar was the full moon, which he knew very well, and there was only one reason he would have been asking. She chewed on the end of her ponytail, staring at his message until the light in the room had shifted. Her tea had gone cold, and she set the mug aside.

Sorry I missed this. I wasn't feeling well last week and took a few days, but I wrote the briefs you asked for. He already had her number, of course, for it was the one she'd registered with HR, but he wasn't going to cross that boundary without her permission, clearly. She bit her lip, hesitating for less than a heartbeat.

Here's my cell if you ever need to reach me about the lunarly account.

She liked having Grayson Hemming chase her, and if she pushed him away entirely, he would find someone new.

Are you feeling better?

The text came early that evening, several hours after she'd responded to his message. Always a question, never a leading statement. He could have said he was glad she was feeling better, and she could have agreed, and that would have been that, but no. He posed questions and waited patiently for their answers, letting her set her own trap. *Typical fucking lawyer.*

She didn't like text messages and phone calls, for neither gave her the upper hand. She needed him to see her, to see her wide eyes and the innocent, girl-next-door look she strove for, her bare legs pulled up with her chin over her knees, the pretty tits he liked concealed under an oversized sorority hoodie. She pulled out her ponytail, ran her fingers through her hair until it was snarl-free, arranged herself against the sofa, and pushed the video icon beside his newly saved number, listening to the song the app played as the call connected, notes like rolling water.

The melody was broken and a small face filled the screen. The little boy had a tumble of dark brown hair that fell over his forehead and bittersweet chocolate eyes fringed in ludicrously long lashes, eyes that widened in shock when they saw her. His mouth opened, perfect little rosebud lips forming a small *oh* of surprise, his head swinging up to the person beside him with a small gasp.

"Well, why did you push the button, buddy?" Her stomach melted at the sound of Grayson's voice, addressing this small child with such familiarity. "Are you going to say hi, or what?" The little boy's eyes swung back to hers, still saucer wide. He mouthed the word 'hi' silently and apparently thought better of it, shaking his head vehemently. "Okay, then give me back my phone, please."

She didn't know why her heart was thumping when he finally filled the screen.

"Talking to girls is at least a kindergarten skill, so you're about a year too early. And before anyone else asks, I do not have games on my phone."

"He's adorable," she laughed, feeling as though someone had taken a plane of sandpaper to her lungs. The little boy *was* adorable, but she hadn't realized he had children, and she didn't like to admit that it changed things. "I am feeling better, thank you for asking."

"I'm glad to hear it."

A face appeared over his shoulder, peering down to examine his call before rolling his eyes, another dark-haired man, a bit younger than Grayson. She heard voices in the background as the man behind him disappeared, the little boy's small voice piping up, speaking to someone out of frame, a woman's voice laughing in response, two loud male voices exclaiming, and then another someone passed behind him. Compared to the silence of her apartment, it was a cacophony, and it was a wonder he could hear her at all.

"I thought maybe you had changed your —"

Something dinged, and she watched a small white shape streak through the frame an instant before Grayson cut off, gasping. His mouth dropped open and his shoulders hunched, and there was an explosion of laughter around him. The phone dropped, forgotten. From the slim vantage point she was afforded, Vanessa watched him launch himself over the back of the sofa with more agility than she'd expected from a man his size, a dozen different voices laughing and shouting, making her wince. The little boy's face appeared again briefly, waving at her silently before jabbing at the screen, disconnecting.

Vanessa blinked, too stunned to process the call. She expected him to be sitting in an equally quiet apartment, tastefully decorated with natural lighting, sipping an old-fashioned without a hair out of place. The noisy, zoo-like atmosphere of wherever he had been did not mesh with everything she knew about him. *And what is that?* Vanessa asked herself. *He's bossy and arrogant and spends a fortune on champagne. That's all you know. You didn't even know he had kids.*

She hadn't expected her phone to go off again that evening, at least not with a call from him. Another video call, much later, when she was already curled in bed. He was as well, his hand propping up his head, his elbow depressing a plump, feather-stuffed pillow. She could see he was bare-chested, the slate grey sheets and modern, minimalist headboard more in line with what she'd expected, and her thighs pressed together, chasing the tingle the sight of him caused.

"Sorry about earlier," he laughed. "I didn't want to leave you hanging with the sight of me covered in egg yolk and no goodbye."

She laughed in spite of herself, feeling a low swoop in her belly. *So what, he has kids. He works such long hours. It's probably joint custody or something, right? It's not like you'd ever have to see them.*

"Is that what that was?! Do I even want to know? Is that your little boy? He's adorable, he looks just like you."

"Oh, no, no thank you. My nephew. I marginally like other people's kids, but I'm allergic to the thought of my own. And no, you really don't want to know."

She breathed in relief. Children had never been a part of her plan, and it didn't matter if people told her she might change her mind down the road. She could see the road clearly, and there were no baby pit stops on it.

"Your brother's? Or sister?"

He chuckled, a low, sardonic sound, shaking his head at her as if she'd unwittingly failed a test she'd not been aware she'd sat for.

"Still as useful as a first-year law student, rabbit. Brothers. I have five brothers, but I didn't call you to talk about any of them."

She pursed her lips. Being on the receiving end of his poisoned tongue at work was expected, and everyone received a piece of his pretentiousness; putting up with it at home was different.

"I just wanted to make sure you're feeling better. I hope the turn didn't take too much out of you."

Despite her annoyance, Vanessa felt as if she were being hypnotized, as if his deep voice's low, velvet roll was putting her in thrall, the sight of him alone in his bed being too delicious to contemplate.

"Maybe next month we can make plans."

She wanted to call him out on it, wanted to call out his hypocrisy, to ask what happened to *nothing would matter once they went back to the office*, but she liked Grayson Hemming chasing her, and she wanted to spend the full moon with him again.

"That would be nice. I'd like that."

The smile he gave her was slow, his lips never parting, but that dimple appeared and her stomach flip-flopped, hoping he would not change his mind.

"Well, I should let you go. See you in the morning."

"See you in the morning," she murmured in agreement, letting out a great whoosh once the phone had disconnected, rolling to her back. There was no way she could go to sleep now, not with his deep voice still humming in her ear, not with the vision of his heavily muscled arm and bare chest dancing in her head. She wondered if he slept naked, if he'd begun stroking himself as soon as they disconnected their call, her hand skating down her body, fingers pressing into her folds to rub at the slickness she found. It didn't take long to reach a shallow orgasm, her fingers and the drone of his voice being enough for her to finish quickly, enough for her to drift to sleep without further thought of him and his infuriating smile.

***

Keeping him chasing seemed to work.

He'd stared at her through the glass the morning after their phone call, his nose wrinkled and his eyes narrowed, their weight staying on her for much of the day. She wondered if he could smell the other man's hands on her skin, the scent of his breath and sweat and semen, and as soon as she got home that evening, she ran a scalding bath. She'd showered multiple times since the moon, of course, but she wanted to be sure. She scrubbed her skin raw, leaving no trace of anything behind other than her soap. It seemed to be enough, for the next day when he watched her, his brows were drawn together, but he'd lost the annoyed look of revulsion.

Several weeks of professionalism, of sharpness and impatience, most of his month spent in the courtroom, and then a text appearing from him the week before the full moon. Plans were made to spend it together. He had an apartment in the Templeton, one of the toniest high-rises in the city, much more in keeping with her initial assumptions. Vanessa tried to remind herself that there was nothing special about being fucked in his bed, for he had undoubtedly fucked countless other women there as well. Still, the bed had been the scene of the crime, and it had felt more intimate than a hotel room.

Her absence the previous month must have still been on his mind as he kissed his way down her body, the smell of another man rankling in his brain for who even knew how long, for despite his previous refusal, once she found herself beneath him, his knot pressed to her insistently.

"I'm going to wear the smell of you like a fucking coat," he groaned into her neck, teeth nipping at her skin with increasing pressure as she clung to his broad shoulders.

When he'd told her he was going to bounce her on his knot that long ago day, she had thought it was vulgar hyperbole, but it turned out to be quite literal. She was splayed over his hips, her knees pressed to the bed, each of his hands gripping her ass, bouncing her on his cock. He brought her down fully on each upward thrust, pressing into the apple-sized knot that had been swollen practically from the moment she'd arrived.

"Every wolf in this city is going to know you belong to *me*, rabbit. My knot is going to smell like your pussy all month long." She squeaked in surprise when he abruptly changed their positions, keeping his cock buried within her as he rolled them to the center of the huge bed. "Up on your knees for me, babydoll. I'm going to fuck you the way I should have from the start."

He pressed into her slowly, pulling her hips back until she was flush to him. His knot kissed the lips of her sex and she whined, once again hating how *good* he felt as he began to rut into her; puzzle pieces that had been carved together from the same imperfect block of flesh.

"This pussy was made for my mouth and my cock, Vanessa. *Mine.* I'm going to lick this pretty little clit and keep you dripping in my cum every month, and there won't be another wolf that can get close to you."

She was on elbows and knees, and he stretched over her, her back pressed to his chest, hips pumping into her ceaselessly. Every thrust was hard and deep, a jolt that rattled her teeth, punctuated by the way his balls slapped into her.

"I should bite you now," he growled against her hair, hips pumping, pushing his nose into the dark tangle until his mouth grazed her shoulder once more, and she whimpered at the thought. He had a hand pressed at her throat, his big, huge hand. His fingers easily spanned the circumference of her neck, tightening with *just* enough pressure for her to feel it, and her blood thrilled at how helpless she was beneath him. "Sink my teeth in and claim you. Is that what you want, rabbit? Are you going to take my knot like a good little bitch?"

"No," she wheezed. His fingers teased her clit, trapping it between his knuckles and pulling until she cried out, his broad fingertips rubbing circles around it that winched her tighter and tighter. "I'm a wolf, Mr. Hemming, not your bitch. I'll bite you back. I'm hot shit, and you need to work for it."

Other wolves would have been angry, she knew without question. The moon made their blood hot and their tempers short, and being rejected by a potential mate wouldn't have been taken kindly . . . but Grayson only laughed, sounding delighted.

"Always with the smart fucking mouth . . ."

The pressure of his cock was unceasing, the slap of his balls as loud as a thunder crack, and soon she was gasping, shaking through her first orgasm of the night beneath him. Vanessa realized he'd been waiting for her to tip over the edge before making good on his promise. The strangled cry that ripped from her throat as his knot popped into place could most certainly be heard in the lobby of the building, eighteen floors below. She moaned again when his teeth sunk into her shoulder, not quite breaking the skin, not claiming her, but hard enough to leave their mark. A deep groan when his cock erupted inside her, his knot pulsing at the lips of her sex as his balls emptied. His fingers were still circling her clit as he pumped, pulling the pleasure out of her until she collapsed under the weight of it. The second, shallower orgasm nearly made her stomach cramp as it ripped through her, and she clenched again around his knot.

"Mmmmm, squeeze me just like that. Your cunt is going to milk me dry."

She felt like an overfilled wineskin when he carefully eased them to the mattress, curling around her protectively. His mouth was hot as he kissed her neck and shoulders, tilting her chin up and back so that he was able to reach her mouth, and the experience was so much different than the other few times she'd let a man do this to her, she thought she might weep.

"What's it like?" she murmured against his skin a short while later, every slight movement causing a tug where their bodies were tied, his knot still swollen within her. "Coming from a family like yours."

She had done her homework since the previous month. She'd known he had a wealthy, connected family when she'd started at the firm; she hadn't realized *how* connected he was, nor that his family basically ruled their own town.

He chuckled against her hair. "The first-year law student learned how to use a search engine, I see." She slapped his chest as he laughed, tugging her infinitesimally closer. "Being a Hemming in Cambric Creek, you mean."

When he didn't respond for a long moment, she sighed. *You should be following his lead. Getting too close doesn't make sense when this is just a work fling.*

"It can be rough." The unexpected rumble of his voice made her jump, and the arm around her tightened.

"Most of the time, it's fine, though. It's whatever. We're living our lives. My dad made sure we had that option." The tips of his fingers skated down the line of her spine with a featherweight pressure, his palm flattening out at the small of her back. "Every once in a while though . . . it can be hard. He told us when we were kids that everyone would be watching, no matter what we did. Watching to take their cues from us, watching us to lead so that they could follow. And then when we screwed up, they'd be there watching with knives."

"Was he right?"

"Oh yeah," he snorted. "He's always right, annoyingly. It is expected that my brother will run for office. It's expected that I'll take the bench. It's a lot of expectations for a small town."

"Is that what you want to do?" she asked, craning her neck to see his expression. "Be a judge?"

"There is *no* money in that, and I have very expensive tastes."

Vanessa laughed, considering his immaculate tailoring, the fine dining and expensive champagne, all the little things about him that whispered quiet luxury. "Yeah, you sure do."

"Do you want to come with me for the turn? I have a cabin out on Shadowbend; it's nice and quiet. It'll ruin you for having to suffer through turning in the city."

"When you put it like that, how can I say no?"

His hand skated down the front of her body, pausing to circle a nipple with his thumb. Vanessa bit her lip as she pebbled beneath his touch, stretching her neck out to push back against him as he gave her other breast the same treatment. His fingers walked down the plane of her stomach, slipping between her thighs and curling into her heat, rolling gently over her clit. He continued to tease and play with her until she was bucking against his hand, the tug of his knot was not as painful as it had been earlier, and when she came against him, his cock slipped free. She'd barely been able to catch her breath once the deluge that spilled from her was cleaned up, for he was hard again and ready for her. Rolling her to her back and hitching her legs over his shoulders, he seated himself to the hilt on his first thrust, as if his cock were sliding home.

It had felt so good that she let him do it several more times that night, and when she sat in the passenger seat beside him as they bumped along a narrow dirt road through the woods that led to the lakeside cabin he owned, she had let him have another first.

***

When she'd been a horny teenager, the thought of shifted sex was a forbidden taboo but one that got her off. She couldn't imagine letting another wolf have her in such a way, and as she grew to adulthood, the idea remained there in the distance, something delicious and dirty that she would probably never experience, one that made her hot all the same.

Everyone experienced the change differently. She knew guru types who taught parallel consciousness workshops, a sort of Tantric training to ensure that one retained their own mind as they shifted, behaving precisely as they would in their human skin, remembering all that happened beneath the moon once they shifted back. She'd never been a particularly good study with esoteric concepts like that. Her time as her other self always felt like a hazy dream, half-remembered and fuzzy around the edges.

She couldn't remember all of the details on how he'd approached her or how they'd reached the patch of moonlight, and she couldn't close her eyes and visualize how the scene must've looked, but her body remembered how it *felt*. She remembered wind in her ears and the sharp, wet smell of the lake, gleefully running from him, making him chase her. She remembered the weight of his body over hers, rolling her against the forest floor, pinning her with his weight, his teeth at her neck and his cock filling her, primal and perfect.

She woke curled against his chest, his fingers tangled in her hair and his arm heavy over her waist, as golden sunlight filtered over the tops of the trees. Her body ached as it always did after the change — bones and muscle knitting themselves back to her familiar form, reshifting and leaving her sore. The aches and pains of transformation were well-known, which was why most businesses allowed lupine employees to take off the day after the moon, but the ache in her muscles was not the only one she felt. There was a sharp pull in her groin every time she shifted, exacerbated when she bent over, the lasting evidence of the way his body had stretched within hers, of what they had done together.

He was still asleep when she woke, and as she nuzzled against his chest, Vanessa was sure they would not go back to the status quo the next day, *could* not go back. She didn't know how to keep him chasing, but there was no way to turn back the clock on what they'd shared.

Forty-eight hours later, as he barked at her over findings that he wanted on his desk, she wasn't sure if she would ever be able to accurately read their situation.

"Let's follow up with Brimm and see where they are with things. Johanna will be forwarding all of the reports to you. I'm meeting with Hastings today, so let's get it done."

She nodded, feeling a bit like his administrative assistant with the way he was once again piling her with paperwork, but simultaneously gratified that she was being called up again to work with one of the larger clients. Hesitating in the doorway, her hands tightened around her tablet, wondering if things were different now.

He glanced up, peering out from underneath a raised eyebrow. “Is there something else you need, Ms. Blevin?”

Vanessa shook her head, pressing her lips together in a tight smile. There was nothing she needed at all, she thought. It was fine, and this is what she should have expected. It didn’t matter what they did or the things he said to her; it didn’t matter if he was constantly sending her mixed messages and signals. He could treat her as callously as he had on her very first day — it was the right way for him to handle the situation. And she would absolutely be blowing him off again the following month, she decided, just to remind him of who was actually in control.

* * *

Chapter Seven

"You're looking at that menu board like it's a case file. Are you waiting for it to talk back to you?"

She scowled, glancing over her shoulder to see he'd never even picked up his head, sunglasses sitting at the tip of his nose as he scrolled through his phone, tapping out a text a moment later.

"Is Trapp's girlfriend going to be there?"

The only one of his brothers she had met at that point was Trapp, a relief, as he was the one who mattered most and was also one of the friendliest people she'd ever known.

She and the small collection of werewolf friends she'd had growing up — made at the pricey werewolf-only summer camp to which her parents made sure to send her and her sibling — had been fixated on pack hierarchies as teens. They were all sheltered suburbanites and didn't know anything about life on the fringes or the reality of pack living; wouldn't know an actual wolfpack if one came through their front doors, but in their hormonal ignorance, they swooned over the idea of a protective, alpha boyfriend, their alpha fantasies growing more x-rated with each successive summer.

Grayson had big alpha energy, as they would have called it all those years ago. He was an aggressive asshole and oozed sex appeal, had the jealousy and protectiveness, and she *hated* that she was falling for an alpha schtick, but her wolf was a pathetic bag of trash for it.

Trapp was altogether different. A sigma wolf, she remembered reading from a magazine, from her position in the top bunk to the assembled girls below, he didn't possess the over-the-top intensity of his two older brothers, had rebuffed the life map that had been laid out for him, had carved out his own little niche in the world, and as a result, he seemed one hundred percent less stressed out than Grayson every day of the week. He was model handsome, with a bright, beaming smile and an easy-going nature, not traits she found particularly exciting for a partner, but excellent in an ally, and she reminded herself as they waited for the coffee that Trapp would be there. It didn't matter if the rest of their ridiculously large family would also be sitting around the table staring at her like a bug — she could focus on the gleaming white teeth belonging to the sibling he was closest with, and hold her breath for the rest of the day.

He took his time answering, never lifting his eyes from the phone. "I'm not sure. I don't know what his plans were for this moon."

Vanessa rolled her eyes so hard that she thought they might get stuck backward in their sockets. Grayson and Trapp each knew what the other was doing every moment of every day, and it was hard to reconcile the fact that *they* were not the twins. Grayson had told her that Trapp was meant to be a doctor, following the roadmap of success laid out for each of them — finance, law, medicine. Jackson, the eldest, had started out following their father's footsteps into the financial world but had taken a right turn into academia, pursuing an economics Ph.D. with a cushy, tenured university position. Trapp had attended a prestigious medical school, had graduated near the top of his class . . . and had quit in the middle of his residency, deciding if he never stepped foot in another hospital, it would be too soon.

"I'm the only one who stuck with the program," Gray had groused, and she'd bitten her tongue to prevent pointing out that his brothers following their own ambitions was not actually a bad thing, and that he was the only one with migraines and high blood pressure, choosing instead to scrape her nails over the endless expanse of his back, distracting him.

"So that means no, because it's not believable that you don't know what he had for breakfast this morning, let alone what he was doing for half the week. You know, it would've been nice not to get into a fight with her when he knew I was coming today. It's actually pretty shitty. That would've been like, the least he could do."

Grayson grinned, tapping out another text but finally lifting his head. "I'll be sure to let him know it was discourteous to not think of you first. I didn't realize you planned to have a bonding experience with the school teacher."

"You say that as if you would last ten minutes in a classroom with even three kids," she grumbled. "Teachers have the hardest jobs there are. But you said she's human, right? That means there would be someone I would rank slightly higher than out of the gate, so yes, it's really shitty of him to have done this."

His laughter was a scraping vibration against her back as he pulled her to his chest, arms crossing over her. "I love the devious way your mind thinks."

She tipped her head back, trying to focus on hearing his heartbeat. *It should be easy to do, considering his shirt is open*. Seeing him this way was incongruous, and even now, months and months later, she still wasn't sure she liked it. Her tightly buttoned-up boss didn't seem to exist in Cambric Creek, and Vanessa wondered what magic the town possessed that stripped away his designer polish so quickly.

He was an early riser, regardless of whose bed he was in. He started his day at sunrise, even the morning after the turn, when they should have been snuggled under the blankets recovering. Instead, she grew used to waking up to an empty bed, the pillow sometimes still holding the depression of his head. When he slept in his own bed in his own house, he was already swimming laps in the icy pool before she even stirred beneath the heavy bedclothes. She had still been curled up that morning, watching a video on her tablet under the covers when he came back into the bedroom, still dripping wet, his hair plastered to his skull.

"Are you watching that fish thing again?"

"It's not about fish," she huffed, screwing her nose up at his dismissive tone. "It's about Bora Bora. Look how pretty . . ." He already knew how crystal clear the water was, for she shoved the travel video under his nose at every opportunity. “Couldn’t we go? You said yourself you’re overdue for a vacation.”

“*I’m* overdue for a vacation,“ he agreed. “Are you planning on coming with me? Because if we’re gone for two weeks, you’ll need to bunk at your desk for the next six months to catch up.”

Rivulets of water ran down his neck, cutting through the dark hair on his chest, and she followed their journey down the plane of his solid stomach, biting her lip as she took in the sight of his cock, soft and full, bouncing against his thigh when he raised the towel to rub at his hair.

His hair had dried that way, sticking out in several odd angles from his head, and most concerningly, he didn’t seem to care. His casual shirt was unbuttoned to the middle of his chest, and he tapped the toe of his topsiders against the leg of the stanchion they stood beside, unselfconscious and uncaring and completely un-Grayson-like.

The coffee shop was a small, independent roaster catering to the town’s multi-species-clientele. He was right, she *had* been looking over the menu board for an interminable amount of time, but there were so many items on it her brain couldn't quite puzzle out, leaving her uncertain if she ought to order something familiar, or take a leap and try something completely new, a decision she was no closer to reaching by the time they had reached the front of the line.

"I'll have a large iced signature roast, max shots, with the bourbon cold foam," Grayson looked at her over the top of his aviators, rolling his eyes when she shrugged helplessly. "And she'll have a large honeycomb latte, hot, and a large iced peach blossom nectar sweet steam."

"I'm never going to be able to drink all that!" she hissed once they had moved to the side of the counter where the drinks would be deposited once made.

Grayson shrugged again. "You didn't know what you wanted, so I figured something familiar and something not. The honey latte is literally just a latte. They make it with a locally sourced honeycomb. And the sweet steam is . . . actually, I don't know what it is, but one of my neighbors is a moth person, and this is what she always orders. Try them both and see which one you like. Save one for later. Throw it at traffic. I don't care what you do, Nessa. Just calm the fuck down."

She scrunched up her nose, scowling at him. It was the *pissy little look* he so often referred to, but at that moment, she didn't care. She was spending the day with his family, the first time she had been invited to do so, a post-moon lunch at his parent's house, and she was a nervous pee-er by nature. Multiple beverages were *not* a good idea.

It seemed as though every conceivable species under the sun called Cambric Creek home, and they were all crowded into the coffee shop at that precise moment. Even though she was not human, she had never lived in a multi-species environment quite like this, she thought, watching an exhausted-looking cervitaur with a snowy-white pelt like a unicorn attempt to come through the doors sideways, behind a pack of fox-tailed young women who never looked up from their phones to realize the traffic jam they were causing.

"And this is like, *normal* for you, right?"

Grayson sighed, pocketing his phone and turning her, taking her hand. "Vanessa. This is where I grew up; it's where my family lives. This is normal because it's home. You need to take a deep breath because you are already wearing me out, and we're not there yet."

"Well, now you're just being mean," she grumbled into his chest, flattening herself against him. She'd not pegged him for a suburbanite, not in the beginning. He was too sophisticated and snobbish, and everything about him whispered luxury and privilege, but she had been wrong. Completely, erroneously wrong, for this other Grayson, who left the house with messy hair and his shirt only half-buttoned, who took up her hand in public and swung their arms carelessly, *existed*. She was able to press her nose against the bare skin the half-open shirt revealed, taking a slow, deep breath, inhaling him.

He kept his apartment in Bridgeton for heavy case-loads, when he was putting in long hours and early mornings, when he needed to be at the courthouse or in chambers or in boardrooms and meeting rooms and coffee shops, meeting nervous clients for the first time who didn't want to come into the office. He used the apartment for hookups, she had no doubt, but unlike those nameless, faceless women she didn't need to concern herself with, she could boast one more thing they could not. He spent every full moon with her, knotted only her, and she was the only one he'd actually taken *home*.

His house was at the rear of a snaking development, too big for a single man, with an expansive front yard and a sloping, cliff-like backyard, upon which he'd spent a small fortune putting in tiered decks and a vast swimming pool. Too big for him alone, but his brother had built a large house, and she had come to understand that anything Jackson did, Grayson did bigger.

All of his siblings lived in town, save for the one who lived overseas, minutes away from each other and their parents. All too soon after leaving the coffee shop, they were pulling into the long, circular driveway in front of an enormous Tudor-style colonial, several other cars already there. She was ready as she would ever be, Vanessa reminded herself. *Here goes nothing.*

***

"Grayson said you're an attorney as well?"

His mother had a spray of freckles across her button nose, and coupled with her vivid green eyes, they gave her a youthful glow, one Vanessa was sure was enhanced by regular enzyme peels and brightening serums and other luxury aesthetic treatments. Her eyebrows were threaded to make them appear natural; her subtle makeup and the expertly applied golden highlights in the cinnamon hair that fell in a waterfall to the center of her back were the same. A whole lot of money and effort to look like no effort was made, and Vanessa knew from her own experience it was the most difficult, costly look to keep up.

"I am," she nodded, meeting the woman's beaming smile. Perfect, even white teeth were shared by the entire clan, and she wondered if the same orthodontist was still in town to give her the same treatment. "Although I've not been practicing for nearly as long as Grayson, especially not in civil law. I started out as a public defender, but the burnout rate is pretty high. I wanted to make the switch before I set myself back any further."

"That is just so smart. Jack, isn't that so smart? I can't even imagine what you had to deal with working for the county, meeting your clients with barely any time to prepare and a system rigged against them. Young attorneys are probably on their knees once they leave the justice center, so smart for you to have moved to private practice. Beauty and brains! Total package. You would be perfect for—"

"Sandi."

His father's voice was mild and even in tone, but his mother cut off, swallowing down whatever effusive praise she had been about to say next, taking less than the space of a heartbeat to recover, giving her another brilliant smile.

"I'm just so happy you're here with us today."

She'd sat at the long table a while later, sipping mimosas and bloody marys, surrounded by a collection of identical-looking men, feeling foolish as a giddy bubble of warmth heated her chest.

"Okay, I need to keep you all straight. So despite being very bossy, Gray is not the oldest—"

"Jackson is the oldest, actually. Gray just doesn't like to acknowledge that," Trapp cut in.

"And he's one with the little boy? Then Grayson, then you."

Trapp nodded, and she watched as Grayson craned his head back surreptitiously, looking into the room where his father and older brother were currently deep in conversation. They were fiercely competitive, unhealthily so, in her opinion, far beyond the typical competition for sports and academic accolades one outgrew before university.

"And then next is . . ." She glanced at the young man sitting across the table. He looked a few years younger than herself, just as handsome as his older brothers, with a much quieter air.

"Hi, I'm Owen. I'm invisible." Beside her, Trapp snorted. "But I'm *technically* not next. That's Lowell. He was only three pounds when he was born, and he still managed to step on me to get out first."

"And he's the one who lives out of the country?"

"Correct," Grayson confirmed, "He is a trainwreck and is currently wreaking his particular brand of bullshit on Tokyo, stars save them. But he travels constantly. He's astoundingly talented." There were several framed examples of his brother's work hanging in Grayson's house, and Vanessa agreed with his assessment. "But . . . yeah, trainwreck. He's both the wreck and the train, simultaneously. A threat to himself and everyone in the vicinity."

"That's so mean!" she laughed, pushing against his thigh. "He's not here to defend himself, counselor."

"It pains me to admit that this is not Gray being an asshole," Trapp chuckled with a wince. "Lowell is like . . . if a hurricane had a baby with an earthquake, and that baby puts sand in your gas tank and then throws a tantrum when you accuse them of doing it."

"Even though he's still holding the bag of sand and conveniently standing over your car."

"Call him," Owen suggested. "Let her see for herself."

"Isn't it the middle of the night in Japan?"

Grayson snorted, ignoring her. The phone rang for only a moment or two before the screen was filled with the glittering eyes of a stupidly handsome young man, bearing the same striking resemblance to Grayson as the rest of his brothers, all looking like younger versions of their father. Lowell talked a mile a minute, was packing for a shoot in Malaysia, seemed entirely unaware of the time, and stood outside on a narrow balcony, a cacophony of fireworks in the background.

"Okay, *he* is a heartbreaker!" Vanessa exclaimed once the call disconnected. The absent brother had a sparkling, frenetic energy about him, one that wasn't as uncomfortably intense as their older brother Jackson's , and bearing no resemblance to Grayson's own icy aloofness. "You're all just jealous! I think he's the cutest one of the bunch, this all makes sense now."

"Yeah, well, careful what you wish for, rabbit. He usually crashes at my place when he comes into town."

"Are you talking about Lowell?" Jack Hemming appeared like a towering spector, leaning on the doorframe. "I hate to be the bearer of bad news, Vanessa, but he's a monster."

It was easy to see where all of his sons got their good looks, and if the first several visits to Cambric Creek had confused her about Grayson, meeting his father cleared up most of the ambiguity. Jack Hemming made her inexplicably nervous. He had a cool confidence and an almost otherworldly air, as though he had ascended this plane of mortal existence and was simply hanging around to bless the small folk with his presence; and although she had never had a thing for older men, had he been the senior partner instead of his son, she likely would have bent over the executive desk sooner, leading to the exact same outcome. He was friendly and terrifyingly charismatic, the sort of person who could convince others to his side with a handful of mildly persuasive words, with a wide smile and shining eyes, but she'd spent enough time around people who excelled at masking to see that behind his smile was the sharp haughtiness she saw every day in his son. His eyes crinkled with his wide smile but never touched them, and she'd had the feeling he was sizing her up the moment her feet first crossed the threshold of his home.

"He's my son, and I love him, but he's the one I most wanted to leave at the bus station."

That time, Vanessa joined in the laughter.

"We had to have two different birthday parties for Lowell and Owen when they were kids. Not two different cakes," he clarified, "not just different cakes and different presents. Two different *parties*, on two different days. For both the family and their friends. Because Lowell didn't want to share his birthday. Can you imagine being a parent at the elementary school and your kid brings home an invitation to not one but *two* parties for twin brothers? Who are in the same grade? Two different weekends you now have to earmark to schlepping your kid across town because these hoity-toity werewolf assholes can't coordinate their kids' parties to be together?"

"You could have said no?" she offered in between her laughter.

"No, you don't understand. You can't say no to him, Nessa," Grayson clarified. "He's a malicious, vindictive little gremlin, and if you say no, he'll put a fork in your microwave. You'll find out the next time he's here."

She wondered if they could tell the heat suffusing her cheeks was from the prospect of him talking about her in the future, or if they would just assume it was from her laughter.

"It's because you have the most patience with him, Gray," his father added, pulling out a seat at the table. "That's why he shows up on your doorstep first. I don't know how you do it, but better you than me."

"I got left off the Christmas card the year we were eight because of Lowell." Owen's voice was somber, and across the table, Trapp's shoulders were already shaking in laughter at the story to come. "And no one realized I was missing until it was too late."

"This is the story you're all going to tell at my funeral, isn't it?" their father sighed.

"So, my mom wanted to do a picture in front of the falls on Main Street, with all the Christmas lights for the card that year," Trapp began. "We'd never done that sort of thing before, and we never did again."

"She went all out for it, too." Jackson had entered the room, grinning when he realized which story was being shared for her benefit. "We had coordinating outfits. Not matching, but coordinated enough to look like we were modeling different looks from the same collection. It took her weeks."

"So we get there," Owen continued, "and there's another family with the photographer, so we have a little lag time. There was a hot chocolate stand at the top of the walkway."

"Out of nowhere, Lowell starts freaking the fuck out." Grayson's voice vibrated against her arm as she leaned into him. "He's writhing around and yelling like he's possessed. Bear in mind, this is during the Christmas Market, so there are people *everywhere*. He had brought his guinea pig, shoved it into his sweater — because that's obviously a great way to treat a guinea pig — and it was scratching his chest."

"Mom tells him to give me the guinea pig and put it in the car, so it doesn't get hurt, and he has a meltdown." Jackson chuckled at the memory as Trapp continued the story.

"Gray volunteers to bring the thing to the car, and then he and Jackson start arguing over this chore neither one of them can complete because Lowell won't give it up. Now he doesn't throw temper tantrums like normal kids. He was that kid who threw the sort of tantrums that made *everyone* in the vicinity stop to watch, you know what I mean? Like, every other parent is feeling sorry for whose ever kid that is, while also feeling really smug that it's not theirs."

"He is howling, Vanessa. Howling like it's the gods damned full moon." She didn't know why everything was funnier in their father's flat, slightly sardonic voice, but she was practically wheezing as he continued. "Screaming that the guinea pig is a part of the family, and if it can't be in the picture, why should he? And is this how the Hemmings treat members of our family? Are we just going to throw him away like we're doing to his guinea pig? This is also the night I started smoking again, I believe."

"Remember what I said about everyone watching?" Grayson added. "It's like the whole damn town was there standing around in the snow that night, watching one of the Hemming kids lose his fucking mind."

"These two idiots are still fighting over bringing the guinea pig to the car," Trapp motioned to his elder brothers.

"Mom told me to bring it to the car," Jackson cut in, before Grayson quickly interrupted.

"But *I* had the keys."

"You only had the keys because you knew I was told to go to the car!"

"And Lowell," Trapp went on, rolling his eyes, "has his arms wrapped around the railing, screaming that he's going to jump in and swim away."

"So I went to get some hot chocolate." Owen's words were enough for her to deduce the rest of the story, and she was laughing too hard to be able to form words.

"Obviously, you see where this is going," Grayson pointed out. "So then dad tells us all that he's bringing us down behind the falls and pushing us into the tunnel back there. You know, like most parents threaten with grounding or time outs, we got 'you'll have to resort to eating each other eventually, and the last one alive will have to survive with the knowledge of what they did,' because that's an extremely healthy thing to say to your kids, after all. And he's Jack Hemming, so he'd probably get away with it."

"So whatever, mom tells Lowell he can hold the stupid guinea pig because, of course, he always gets his way, and the tears turn off like a switch. He is just fucking *beaming* in this picture. The photographer tells my mom she should have the finished prints back in a week or so," Trapp continued, "but here's the sheet of digital proofs for her to look over in the meantime, to decide what sort of package she wants to buy."

"She's staring at this little thumbnail, and she's counting." Grayson's laughter was rough and deep, twisting something in her core, making her want to drag her nails up his thighs. "She's counting because she knows something doesn't look right, but she can't figure out who's missing. Then Owen comes wandering up like he's been hanging out with someone else's family, drinking his hot chocolate, and dad refuses to do the whole thing over again, so we leave."

Everyone was laughing too hard at that point to continue, everyone but Owen, who shook his head in disgust.

"You assholes didn't even know I was gone."

As they left, his mother gave her a tight hug, saying she hoped they would see her the following month, giving Grayson a pointed look as he bent to kiss her cheek. As they pulled out of the development, Vanessa wondered silently if he would invite her again or if that would seem too much like catching.

***

They went back to Bridgeton after leaving his parents' house, an oddly domestic tableau that flipped her stomach with equal parts wanting and dread, but she stretched against him in the center of his big bed all the same, not ready to go back to her apartment and work and the reality that in the morning she would be just another one of the attorneys who worked under him. She *liked* knowing that there were two Graysons, liked knowing she was the only one with the knowledge, almost as much as she liked him chasing.

"Do you think they liked me?"

She wasn't sure why it was important to her. It wasn't as if she was going to be granted some sort of VIP induction into the Hemming wolfpack based on the singular strength that she was fucking their son, but she liked seeing a slightly softer side of him, liked the family she had met, and understood him so much better.

"Of course they did," he murmured, his voice already heavy with sleep. "You're perfect. Are you staying the night, or are you leaving?"

"What do *you* want me to do?" she asked, nuzzling against the side of his chest. Indecision was not a hat she wore well, nor was submission, but perhaps she, too, had two sides in Cambric Creek.

"It doesn't make a difference to me, but if you're going to stay, you can jerk me off so I can get to sleep. I'm leaning towards that option at the moment."

Vanessa raised her head, scowling. She was wrong. There was only one Grayson, she corrected, and he was the fucking worst. She continued giving him her *pissy little look*, but his eyes were closed, a lazy half smile on his face, and she knew he wasn't joking. His cock had thickened as he laid naked beneath her — thick but not yet hard. He groaned when her nails dragged over his groin as she shifted down the bed, scratching against the base of his shaft. When she lifted it, pumping his foreskin and relishing the weight of it in her hand, he melted into his pillow.

"Yes, you should definitely stay."

"Are you sure this is all you want?"

He lifted his head again, squinting down at her. "I'd love a blowjob, but I have an early meeting. I can't be up all night while you dry heave all over my—" He cut off on a choked gasp when she gripped his testicles, twisting slightly.

"If you're as smart as you think you are, you'll stop while you're ahead." Vanessa grinned at his obedient silence, continuing to pump him slowly until his slit winked against his shiny pink tip. She slid her tongue into his foreskin, stretching the sheath of flesh away from his head and rubbing its sensitive interior before sliding it down gently and releasing his cockhead with a *pop*.

"This feels like a very lopsided arrangement, Mr. Hemming."

"Then climb up here and let me suck on your clit. But be quick about it, rabbit, because I really am tired."

"I honestly can't stand you."

She cupped his balls as she continued to pump his shaft, rolling his fat testicles in her palm, giving each one a bit of stretch. *Still want to step on them sometimes.* Straddling his face and letting him put his tongue to work *did* sound appealing, but she had to admit, she was also tired, and the roiling heat that had gripped her the previous several days had been thoroughly extinguished.

Besides, Vanessa was forced to admit to herself — she liked taking care of him this way. His heavy cock would stiffen to steel, her loose movements becoming focused, thumb pressing into his frenulum on every pull, pushing into his root on every downstroke until he was groaning. She liked the moment when he came, the first burst of semen rolling over his cock head onto her hand, while the second and third would be powerful spurts, ropes of white that would land on his chest and belly if she allowed them, the rest pooling at the base of his cock and running over her knuckles.

“Such a paragon of romance. Whatever, this is fine. But you gotta make it up to me this week.”

His huge hand palmed her head, thumb tracing over her jaw with more tenderness strictly required for a handjob, and her heart thrummed. *It doesn’t matter. Stop thinking it matters.*

“I wouldn’t expect anything less, Ms. Blevin.”

* * *

Chapter Eight

2 Years Earlier. . .

She didn't expect Grayson to suddenly decide she was the love of his life; didn't expect him to put her above work, and a certain measure of freedom had come with her lack of expectations.

She no longer stayed home counting the days between full moons, knowing he wasn't either. She had precious little free time as it was, and spending it pining over someone who was not doing the same over her felt like time poorly spent. It didn't lessen her enjoyment of the time spent with him, and there was no one else with whom she wanted to spend the full moon, no one else with whom she wanted to spend any full moon ever again.

She wasn't interested in being knotted and claimed by another wolf, and if it wasn't the annual Lupercalia celebration, she had precious little patience for their bluster and machismo. He was the only one who would knot her, the only one with whom she shared the turn, and if the smell of another man's touch on her skin made him go cross-eyed in jealousy every once in a while, Vanessa had decided that simply wasn't her problem.

She liked having Grayson Hemming chase her, but she had determined that if the goalposts were never moved, he would grow tired of the game.

***

The swell of skin was molten beneath her lips, hot and slick from her mouth. Her tongue traveled up a pulsing vein, pausing to suck until his stomach muscles jumped beneath her palm. She increased the pressure, sliding her tongue over him, lips tightening, the sound of his heavy panting like a symphony above her.

Vanessa smiled as she pulled back, sucking until the moment she released, letting her lips pop. When she replaced them with the blunt edge of her teeth, scraping lightly against the bulb of flesh, his heavy pants coalesced into a choked grunt. His chest heaved as she dragged her canines over his knot, pressing just enough to make it hurt. She loved this period, just before the moon, when he was oversensitive and his knot swelled up as soon as his cock got hard, and she could make it hard so easily.

"I'm going to fuck that smile off your face, Vanessa," he choked out, his big hands fisting in the sheets. "I'm going to pump you with my knot, over and over again until you're gaping. I'm going to . . . fucking . . . *ruin* you for anyone else."

She laughed, delighted by the way he was wheezing, biting harder. She had learned several important lessons over the last year. That he was *not* quiet was one of her favorites. She could pull grunts and groans from his throat with ease, and the sound he made when he came — his balls emptying in thick, white ropes across her breasts and belly, spurting into her mouth, running down her thighs as he erupted into her — made her legs tremble, like a Pavlovian response. He had a deliciously filthy mouth, but *this* — his strangled moans and wheezing pants, the empty threats, and the teeth-gnashing tantrum he threw every time he wasn't in absolute control — had become some of her favorite sounds in the world.

It was a relief being out of the office. She'd found herself regularly ducking into corners and empty conference rooms to breathe, to remind herself that big law was full of personalities like his, that he wasn't even the only overbearing asshole at *this* firm. She noticed he tended to get stuck in litigation mode, particularly when juggling multiple big clients with pressing needs. Aggression and combativeness were highly valued traits in the courtroom. That was what brought clients to the door... but those same traits were a nightmare in the office. Now though, they were free, and she intended on paying him back for the warpath he'd been on for the past two weeks.

Dragging her nails down the meat of his thighs until she knew she would leave welts, visible marks of her ownership of every inch of him, Vanessa pushed herself to her knees, fastening her lip around his cock and swallowing as deeply she was able, which was embarrassingly little, relishing the rumble in his chest nonetheless. That he would let her do whatever she wanted to him was another lesson, one she exploited at every turn.

"I'm sorry," she crooned, running her tongue over his weeping slit, sucking up the pre-cum pearling at the tip, "we haven't been very nice. Is this better, baby?"

He groaned again when she resumed sucking his cock to the best of her meager abilities. He could palm her head with ease, and he did so as his fingers tightened in her hair, shallowly thrusting upwards into her mouth.

"How can someone have such a smart fucking mouth and still be so bad at sucking cock?" His voice was a rasp, and he rumbled when she dug her nails into the side of his thigh before slapping his skin.

"Does that mean I should stop?" she choked out, gasping for air, a line of drool connecting her mouth to his swollen glans. He was right. He loved having his perfect, porn-worthy cock sucked, and she was ridiculously, horrifically bad at it, possessing both a strong gag reflex she could not overcome and a jaw that tired quickly. It seemed like a waste, being involved with someone like her.

"Did I say that?" he laughed, pushing the fingers of one hand through her hair and gripping her chin with the other, tracing her lower lip with the edge of his thumb before guiding her mouth back to him. "It's alright. You're perfect, baby. I'm still going to ruin you, but I love your worthless, terrible mouth . . ."

She was stretched too full to be able to smile, humming over the backhanded sentiment as he continued to mutter obscenities and misplaced appreciation. The thought of him being with other women still caused a ripple of fury to move up her back, but she knew they existed, just as she saw men who were not him in those meaningless weeks between moons, and she only hoped the partners he had throughout the month who were not her were sucking his beautiful cock the way it deserved.

***

She'd witnessed it once at the prior year's Lupercalia celebration. Two girls on the veranda, humans both, on their knees before him as he reclined on one of the chaise lounges, servicing the thick rod of flesh that routinely made her gag. She'd frowned at the sight of them, particularly the blonde who'd been deep-throating him with ease, as if she'd had her back molars removed, along with her tonsils and uvula, while a petite redhead sucked his testicles.

"Overindulging?"

He'd smiled lazily with a shrug, a quicksilver gleam in his heavily hooded eyes, beckoning her over.

"I didn't know where you'd gotten off to. These guests looked lonely, and let it not be said I'm not a gracious host."

He'd caught her earlier that night, had taken her on hands and knees, and she'd only been slightly mortified at being had in public, her first Lupercalia with him only taking place the year before. Afterward, she was lost to the tidal wave of hedonism, allowing another wolf to swing her around the waist, bending her over and entering her from behind.

"I don't want to be a third wheel . . ."

"Don't be stupid," he'd cut her off, gripping her wrist and pulling her to recline beside him. "They were bored, and you weren't around. Two mouths are better than one, rabbit."

His teeth had tugged at her pout, his tongue sliding against her, lips trapping lips in soft suction. She gasped when his mouth trailed over her jaw and throat, teeth catching at her clavicle before he kissed over her shoulder. Hot need, his mouth was demanding and reverent, sucking at her pulse point and kissing the hollow of her throat before reversing course to crash back into her lips with renewed urgency. She couldn't suck his cock like this human, and she wasn't the only woman he fucked, but she was the only one he knotted, the only one with whom he shared being a wolf, and the only one he kissed this way.

She realized how close he was when he'd growled against her lips. His hips thrust upwards into the woman's mouth in a quick, steady rhythm, gripping her high ponytail to direct her movement.

"Where do you want me to finish, rabbit?"

She could have said anything, could have said anywhere. She could've instructed him to line up both of the girls and paint their faces in thick gobs of white release, could have ordered the blonde not to waste a single drop, to lick it from her companion. But they were humans, she'd reminded herself. He had a pitifully low opinion of humans, his father's rhetoric, she'd quickly learned, one she found herself internalizing more and more. *They* were superior, and neither of these girls was worthy of a single drop.

"In my mouth," she breathed against his lips, her heart somersaulting when he smiled, kissing the tip of her nose before pulling out of the blonde's mouth and pushing to his feet. The girl was gasping. Vanessa tightened her lips around the flared edge of his cockhead when it bumped her lips, using her tongue to lave at him as he erupted with a groan. Her smile may have been smug when she finally released him, but she'd reminded herself that this was *their* holiday, and the humans were seat fillers. *We all have our parts to play.*

***

Unfortunately for him, he was stuck with her now, not that her sloppy technique and minimal ability seemed to matter much to him just then. He had both hands on her head now, fingers through her dark hair, holding her in place as his hips did the work. She let him fuck her mouth for several minutes more, able to tell from his breathing when he was close. He was *not* finishing this way, not after she put in so much effort working him up, for, despite his strangled threats, he had let her edge his cock for close to an hour.

Vanessa understood *why* he was such an asshole; that privilege led to the expectation of more privilege, for she now felt that she possessed an all-access pass to his body, free to do whatever she wanted to him, whenever she wanted to do it. His stomach was slick from the pool of pre-come he'd been drooling, his balls tight and sensitive, and she decided, with one last, sucking kiss to his swollen, purple head, that she had tortured him enough. His poor, oft-abused brain could use the dopamine hit, and she wanted to feel him explode inside her.

The meat of his shaft slid between her thighs as she swung her leg over his hips, fitting in the cleft of her cunt as if he belonged there, which she supposed he did.

"Don't threaten me with a good time if you don't mean it, Mr. Hemming."

He managed to push himself up, somehow going from his back to his knees without dislodging her, impaling her on his cock in one slow thrust. Vanessa dropped her head back when his hips began to move, and she whimpered when his teeth grazed her throat, her eyes feeling as if they were spinning in her skull as his girth dragged over her g-spot. It was one of her favorite positions — all the benefits of cowgirl, bouncing on the fat length of him, feeling his knot press against the mouth of her cunt on every thrust, not quite breaching, but providing the delicious threat of doing so, and best of all — she didn't need to do any of the physical work. He held her up, his hips moving like a machine, allowing her to enjoy the pleasure with none of the strain.

She gasped when he hit something inside her, some hidden spot in her anatomy that only he'd ever been able to reach in such a way, and he chuckled. "Right there?"

"Right there," she agreed on a wheeze, moaning when he continued to hammer into the same spot.

"Right there, then." He groaned when she squeezed him, fingers digging into her ass. His eyes were closed, his head tipped slightly back, and she wondered if she shared his slightly blissed-out expression, confident that she did.

"Just like that . . ." He rolled a finger against the hood of her clit, slowing the movement of his hips. Every time her pelvic floor contracted in pleasure, he groaned against her hair, relishing the clench of her muscles. He rubbed her clit and she squeezed his cock, earning the gift of that throaty little moan in response, a cycle she'd be happy to continue endlessly. "Squeeze me just like that, baby." His face dropped against her neck, and for a moment, Vanessa couldn't quite remember what he'd done to earn his punishment. "Hold me tight, rabbit. I love your pussy so much . . . This tight little pussy was made for my cock."

"She loves your big cock," she keened in agreement, going cross-eyed from the way he was dragging over that spongy spot within her, hitting the side of her cervix in a way that turned her lungs inside out instead of stabbing at it painfully.

She was forced to admit that he knew how to use it. She'd been with well-endowed guys before who seemed to think the size of their cocks would make up for their lack of bedroom skill, but Grayson instinctively knew how to move within her, how to best twist and contort her body to feel the rub of his girth on the most sensitive parts of her anatomy until her spine turned to jelly and she was unable to support herself, stretching her open and filling her completely, even in the weeks when his knot wasn't a factor.

Which was, she thought, as his fingers rolled over her clit, causing her stomach muscles to seize up as she cried out, the most important lesson of all. The moon's position in the sky had very little to do with their appetite for each other, and they had dispensed with the pretense of this being limited time diversion.

The pressure of his knot, like an overinflated balloon teasing entrance at her lips on every thrust, made her squeak like a toy when he began to fuck her in earnest, his hips snapping. The first sparks of light made her dizzy, the promise of relief, to cool the fire in her blood and ease the ache she felt for him, and she flailed, wanting to race towards the light.

"I'm so close," she gasped, tightening her arms around his shoulders, feeling the first shivers of her impending climax shaking her legs.

"What was that, rabbit? I didn't quite catch that." Abruptly, he stopped moving, the pressure she needed vanishing. She gaped for several interminable heartbeats, the sparks ebbing away, the tide of her orgasm receding. His deep chuckle, when she tightened her grip on his shoulders, was gleefully malevolent.

"Grayson, I swear to the mother, if you don't keep going . . ."

"Mmmmm," he hummed against her temple, moving a hand to lightly grip her throat, tracing her lips with the tip of his thumb. "Always with the smart mouth and the pouty little sneers," he murmured, kissing her forehead as if she were a porcelain doll. She needed him to move, needed friction against her clit and the full pressure of his cock thrusting within her, but all he did was run a light fingertip down her sternum, circling her nipple and gently cupping her breast. "You always have to be right, Vanessa; that's the problem. You push, and you pull like it's going to accomplish something, and you're still operating under the delusion that you're in charge. This is why we can't have nice things."

She slowly let out the breath she'd been holding and closed her eyes. He was a bossy asshole, and he wanted to dominate her. All she had to do, she reminded herself peevishly, was let him.

"Tell me what you want, rabbit. All you have to do is ask."

Dragging her nose against his throat, she peppered the sharp edge of his jaw with tiny kisses. She loved how he smelled and would never be able to smell another person in the whole world; she was sure of it. She loved the heat of his body and the solidity of it against hers, the change already boiling his blood. Tightening her thighs around his hips to pull him closer, she wondered if it would never feel close enough. *This is how he always wins.*

"I want you to fuck me like you mean it."

He hummed against her skin. "Is that all?"

Such a fucking asshole. She gritted her teeth. "I want you to make me come." She was not good at being subservient and knew she'd never last a single evening at one of those sex clubs in the city. She loved feeling helpless beneath him when her muted heat made her blood sizzle, and his scent overwhelmed her, but *that* was different. Grayson cocked his head consideringly, that godsdamned dimple making another appearance.

"No, I don't think I will," he mused. His teeth grazed the shell of her ear, nipping at the tender skin, his breath hot at her neck. "Not until you beg."

"Grayson—"

"The choice is yours, rabbit. You like being in control so much, right? Well, you have the freedom to pick what happens next." Two thick fingers pressed into the side of her clit, circling with the infuriating precision of someone who'd done so a million times before, who knew exactly how to take her to pieces. Her eyes fluttered closed as he moved against her rhythmically, not exactly the way she wanted to come, but coupled with the press of his cock within her, it would be enough.

When the movement of his fingers stopped as abruptly as he'd ceased thrusting, she moaned in frustration.

"*Please* make me come."

He chuckled against her throat, a smug, self-satisfied sound, and she was tempted to elbow him in the jaw. He rolled his hips against her though, thrusts that hit just the right spot, and her head tipped back in ecstasy . . . until he stopped once more.

"How?"

"Grayson," she choked out, tightening a hand in his hair until she could feel it pull against his scalp, "*please* make me come. Please fuck me, *please* give me your knot. Please make me come before I rip your *fucking* throat out, you smug piece of shit."

His shoulders were shaking in laughter against her, jostling her against him until he tightened his grip on her ass, hitching her legs tighter around him. The first roll of his hips made her gasp, hitting her in a way that made her head drop back. She could feel every inch of his meaty shaft spreading her wide, each drag against her enough to reignite the spark of her peak.

"Is this what you need, baby? Let me give you exactly what you want."

Her eyes popped open when he surged upward without warning, his knot popping into place within her, her mouth dropping open in a silent scream.

He groaned into her hair, hips rolling against hers once more in a steady thump. With every thrust, she felt the tug and push of his knot, fucking in and out of her, pleasure that bordered on pain, but it was an *exquisite* pain. She began to feel the buzzing tremors shiver up her legs once again, the solid pressure of him being enough to bring her back to the edge . . . Until he pulled his knot from her completely, his cock bouncing in the air beneath her body, leaving her gasping. She cried out, clawing at his neck, her legs kicking out as though she were being electrocuted.

"This *is* what you wanted, isn't it, rabbit? Don't threaten you with a good time? How am I supposed to deny you anything when you ask so sweetly, baby?"

He pushed in again, and even though she was sure she would be gaping open from the treatment, the thickness of his cock and the swollen ball of flesh at its base filled her completely, sealing her shut.

"Tell me what you want, rabbit."

Heat flooded her veins, a fire that had nothing to do with his knot, the embarrassment and anger she'd felt all week returning to her in a rush. "I don't ever want you to talk to me that way again, like I'm some inept intern. Especially in front of people. Do you understand me, Gray? *Never* again. That's what I want."

She'd not been the only victim of his black mood that week at work, but his sharp dressing down had still stung, particularly in front of junior team members, young attorneys who sat where she'd been only a few years earlier. She'd rewritten the brief he'd flung back at her, had been extra diligent with every bit of work that crossed her desk the rest of the week, and the first break she'd had, she texted her most satisfying hookup option.

She was diligent about safe sex with every partner who wasn't him, and she knew her actions were fueled by pure malice, spite the only thing keeping her exhausted body upright. She had let her hookup partner ejaculate all over her breasts and belly, the pretty tits he loved so much, smearing her finger's in the other man's release and opting to skip her shower when she got home that night. The smell had turned her stomach as she'd sat at her desk the next day, but the sight of the vein bulging above Grayson's eye, his tight fists and his furious expression had made it worth it.

His eyebrow raised, fingernail tracing her jaw. "Are we talking about work now?" His lips lowered, kissing the tip of her nose, and her nostrils flared. "Then don't ever turn in such shit work again. There's nothing I can do with a garbage brief, so if you don't want to be treated like an inept intern, don't fucking act like one." He kissed her again, her fists balling at her sides. "And don't ever come to my bed smelling like another man's cock again."

He'd already begun to turn, pivoting to the inside of the bed, his hips already bucking upward. Her nails raked down his back for purchase, gripping his hair, ready to sob if he didn't finish her off.

"Who does this perfect pussy belong to, Vanessa?"

"Yours," she wheezed. "It's yours. It belongs to you."

She felt herself tipping, tightening her legs around him and gripping his hair as she squealed, her back hitting the center of the mattress. He kept them tightly pressed together so that his knot did not pull out of her again. When he began to move against her with deep, solid rolls that kept them fused, she was done. Her climax shook through her like an earthquake, the epicenter at her core, where their bodies were connected. Her muscles contracted around him so tightly it was nearly painful, and she imagined being strong enough to rip his cock from his body. She would practice her kegels every day, would tighten and hold at her desk as she wrote his precious fucking briefs, and someday she'd squeeze him hard enough to reduce him to pulp. If she belonged to him, then he belonged to her, so it was only fair, she rationalized.

She felt the moment when his orgasm rippled up his spine, the familiar groan making her legs shake as his cock went off like a geyser, filling her with spurt after spurt of molten heat, her belly bulging again. He punctuated each pulse of his balls with a short roll of his hips, emptying into her. When his cock finally spat up the last of his release, he rolled her carefully, and the sloshing pressure within her was nearly enough to make her come again.

When he knotted her from behind, he would carefully ease them until he could lay flat on his back, her body splayed over him, rubbing slow circles over her clit until she was panting and bucking against his hand. The tug of his knot increased her pleasure, and the clenching contractions of her orgasm as he rubbed her to completion made his cock hard within her until his knot slipped free, and he fucked her all over again.

When he knotted her from the front, however, he kissed her. Vanessa had come to determine that the reason kissing him had been absent from all of her early fantasies was that anything she conjured up in her head wouldn't have been able to compete with the reality of his teeth nipping at her lips and throat, and the slow slide of his tongue against hers. She would be pressed to his broad chest, nails dragging through the dark hair that lightly covered his sculpted pectorals, the thump of his heartbeat lulling her sated body to sleep, curled against him with a heavily muscled arm draped over her. When she woke, he would fuck her slow and deep, tilting her pelvis so that he rubbed against her clit, hilting himself within her on every thrust until her heartbeat matched the thump of his hips, and she shook apart beneath him.

"You make everything so difficult," he grumbled into her hair, and she shook her head resolutely.

"I'm not the one who made things difficult. Not at all." She curled against the broad plane of his solid chest, cradled in his arm, held tight and close. They'd not be going anywhere anytime soon.

"You belong to *me*." His voice was a whisper against her hair, and she tightened her arms, shaking from the force. Every once in a while, despite her best efforts, he caught her. "Don't forget it, rabbit."

* * *

Chapter Nine

1 YEAR EARLIER . . .

She'd known something was wrong the moment she woke. She felt sluggish and heavy, with a slight wave of nausea and mild vertigo as she staggered to the bathroom to empty the contents of her stomach. She'd felt an itch in her skin the entire day at work, and when the next day brought more of the same, she stopped at the corner pharmacy on her way home that evening, a heavy stone of certainty sitting in her stomach.

When she arrived back at her apartment, she deposited her bags on the counter — Chinese takeout, a bag of fun-size caramel candies that had made her mouth water at the sight of them when she stood in the pharmacy's checkout line, and a collection of pregnancy tests. As she stood before the aisle in the store, she thought about how important the work they did was.

Hastings—Durning Pharma, one of the only multi-species pharmaceutical companies on the market, recreated common over-the-counter medications and remedies for a non-human clientele. He still treated her as he always had at the office, the same sneering pompousness with which he treated everyone, but she had been brought along on the meetings with one of the firm's biggest clients, *his* biggest clients.

She'd been brought along and introduced, slowly eased on board as a part of their team, and now she was meeting with their representatives independently. It was the singular professional gift he'd given her, but a mighty one, she recognized. It was not her account, and they were not her clients, but it was a far cry from stacks of discovery documents on her desk and a box of highlighters. They liked her. They said so every time they met, opining that they were grateful Grayson had left them in good hands in his absence for the afternoon.

The red tape was endless. Nothing underscored how completely the scales were tipped for humans when a basic OTC antihistamine for nonhumans had to go rounds of battles to be approved by the federal regulatory committee. With each month that passed, Vanessa found herself in longer and deeper conversations with Grayson's father, deciding his werewolf-first way of thinking was not as radical as she had initially thought. She was still a tiny fish in their pond, and she knew the meetings she was left to steward weren't of any real consequence, but it was a stepping stone to building a relationship with this client.

There was nothing on the shelf in the pharmacy made for her. Four different brands of pregnancy tests for humans, one for nagas and lizardfolk, and nothing else. She put three of the four options for humans on the counter, along with the bag of candy and a bottle of water, leaving with her heart in her mouth. She realized that Cambric Creek would likely have what she was looking for, but she dared not venture to his mother's doorstep for this particular task.

Halfway through her mu shu pork, three plus signs gracing the wands currently perched at the edge of her tub, she looked up the number for the clinic in Starling Heights. They were a family planning clinic exclusively for werewolves, Moon Blood something or other. She remembered seeing advertisements on the train and easily found the listing for their number. There was nothing else to be done.

She had a roadmap, and there were no pit stops for babies or motherhood on it that she could see. She liked knowing she was doing work for an organization in existence for people like her. She had made her billable-hours quota every year she'd been with the firm, was a junior associate no longer, and the ladder before her only went up. She didn't mind the long hours, didn't mind the resulting lack of a substantial social life, and there was no room to be responsible for someone else. She'd fallen asleep while using the restroom just the week prior, leaving her desk around 10:15 p.m. to visit the lavatory down the hall, waking with a start nearly two hours later, her head sliding against the side of the stall until she'd nearly fallen forward off the toilet, yelping to wakefulness. That was what big law was; that was what she'd chosen. She was happy with her choices and liked her life precisely as it was.

Maybe she would change her mind someday, Vanessa allowed. She might look back on this decision with bittersweetness, and perhaps she would change her mind, but it was not this day. She had no intention of doing this and certainly not alone.

She didn't need to ask to know what he would have said. He liked his life as well. He didn't want children, he'd said so before, on more than one occasion, and she'd not put him in the position of being the one to tell her what to do. He kept things quiet and dark, left his expensive cufflinks where small hands would be able to reach and swallow, and tolerated his little nephew in small bursts. Perhaps he, too, might change his mind in the future, if they had a future that included each other, but it would not be this day.

She called the clinic the following morning, made the earliest appointment, and took the rest of the week off work. She could already smell the difference in her urine and didn't want him smelling it on her, for she knew it would change everything, just as the thought of him having children had nearly changed things for her all those moons ago.

She'd had brunch with his family more times than she could count, celebrating the full moons and their shared nature, celebrating what they were together. She understood the dynamic he had with his brothers, understood the fraught dynamic they all had with his father. Part aggravation, part hero worship, and very easily manipulated, although she would never tell him that. Still, her observations of his family over the better part of the last two years had given her insight on Grayson that she never would have gleaned in the courtroom, the office, or beneath him in his bed.

Jack Hemming was an island. He permitted his wife and sons temporary mooring at his shoals, one at a time, but behind the genial smile and cooly affable personality, Vanessa saw the machinations and planning, a permanently guarded heart, and his son was exactly the same.

She liked to claim she wore her heart on her sleeve and cultivated the wide-eyed passion necessary to make the assumption stick. Utter bullshit, of course, but it was useful for taking opposing counsel and judges by surprise, although Grayson had never once fallen for her schtick. He wore his heart on his sleeve as well — pulled up, concealed under sleeve after sleeve of high-end cotton and french cuffs, pricey champagne and a revolving door of women whose names he barely bothered learning, layers and layers, his heart pinned somewhere at the center, and she had abandoned the expectation of ever truly reaching it.

And when she really scraped down to the heart of things, she hadn't let him in very far either. She'd not brought him home to meet her family, had never alluded that she was seriously involved with anyone. The thought of admitting aloud for the whole world to hear that she had begun a sexual relationship with her boss made her skin crawl. It didn't matter if she couldn't bear the smell of other men, an affliction that had cut her mid-month extra-curriculars in half, and it didn't matter if he was the only wolf she ever wanted to spend another full moon with for the rest of her life. She didn't feel any closer to knowing what he wanted than she had the day she'd let him follow her to that hotel lobby. Vanessa wasn't sure if she quite knew herself, but that was a reflection for another day. Neither of them was fit for this, not at present, and she'd not make their dysfunction someone else's problem.

***

When she returned to work, she barely noticed his absence at first. It was not unusual for him to not be in the office, and several days passed before she realized he was not at trial, was not busy with meetings, and was just as absent as she had been for the week and a half prior.

The house was black when she arrived. Blackout curtains kept the bedroom shrouded in darkness, the temperature was set to a near Arctic degree, and she found him exactly where she thought she might — on his back in the center of the bed, a tight skullcap over his head that extended over his eyes, one she knew was an ice pack.

"Hi, baby," she whispered. She crawled onto the edge of the mattress, attempting not to jostle him. "Can I call someone? Can I bring you anything? Tell me what you need."

One of his fingers hooked around hers, pulling her hand closer, shaking his head infinitesimally.

"Trapp is on his way," he whispered, the slightest exhalation of air. "How was your trip?"

Her lungs seized, and she threaded their fingers together. She'd told him she was going home to visit her family, someone's birthday, and he had accepted it without question. She would tell him the truth, she had decided, but not now. She would wait until he was upright and no longer in pain; until the crampiness had passed from her body and he was back to barking at her in the office, then she would tell him what she had done, the decision she had made that affected her and only her, that would have ended them.

She watched a needle slip into his skin; Trapp seeming as chipper as ever, utterly unfazed by his brother's condition.

"You know, between the debilitating neurological condition of his brain attempting to chew its way free a few times a month and his blood pressure, he's probably going to drop dead of a stroke before he's forty-five," he told her cheerfully as she walked him out of the dark house. "So if you're planning on tricking him into marrying you, I'd start planning the ceremony."

"Trapp! That's horrible!" she scolded. "I'm going to tell your mom you said that. Has-has he always been like this?"

"Oh yeah, since we were kids. He had a second bedroom behind my dad's office because that was the one room of the house that was completely off-limits, and even Lowell knew better than to disobey. So it was the one place that could be kept dark and quiet. Are you staying, or do I need to come back to check on him?"

"No, I'm staying," she decided at that moment. She'd call in again tomorrow if necessary. *It's not like you're going to get in trouble for it.*

"He needs to go to the ER if there's no improvement in the next few hours. You have my number, right?" She nodded, watching him swing into the huge truck, the emblem of the town's firehouse on the door. "Call me if it gets to that point. I'll start writing my best man speech, but I can't promise it's not going to be really embarrassing."

She swallowed several painkillers she'd received from the clinic before tiptoeing back to the bedroom and curling up at his side, gratified when his hand found hers, threading their fingers again. She began to knead at the flesh of his palm, a reflexology video she'd watched a hundred times burned into her brain. She didn't know if it actually helped him any more than the human-strength Tramadol she'd carried in her bag for him for the better part of the last two years, but it made her feel better to try.

It had been a very long week, and she wanted to put it behind them. Sometimes they both needed a break from the chase, she thought, closing her eyes, breathing him in.

* * *

Chapter Ten

Fuck in his office every time he's horny didn't have quite the same ring to it as *getting it out of our systems*, but two years later, it seemed far more accurate. And probably not entirely fair, she was forced to admit, for he made sure to take care of her needs just as frequently.

She already knew they were the source of some gossip. Vanessa was confident that no one would've ever overheard them in his office — his suite was separated by an outer office, Johanna the only potential audience to their mid-day rendezvous, but she suspected that his longtime assistant had known from the beginning. She always had legitimate reasons for traveling up to the executive floor, particularly once she was made part of the Hastings–Durning team. He was never anything but short with her, the same as he was with everyone, their on-the-clock behavior, to all who may have been looking, completely commonplace.

She suspected someone must have seen them out together. Sharing an intimate table for two at one of Bridgeton's high-priced restaurants, or perhaps stepping out of his car at the curb in front of the Templeton. Someone must have seen something, and she knew from experience that was all it took.

She was used to being someone with an inside track on company gossip, no matter where she worked. She made a point of being friendly with the biggest blabbermouths, never trusting them, but keeping them close enough to hear what secrets they were eager to share. She would befriend the cleaners and the mail clerks, invisible presences who always knew the dirt on the bosses, knew which coworker was getting sacked or who was pregnant, or who was humped over the broken printer in the supply room.

Now things were different. When she walked into her room, conversations halted. Eyes followed her, averting quickly when she looked up. The moment she stepped out of the doors, the whispers began again, often punctuated with giggles.

She had decided not to care. She was a mid-level associate on her way up the ladder and had begun optimistically researching the salary caps on the SA1 and SA2 positions within the firm. She worked on holidays, worked on weekends, spent more nights at her desk than she did in her bed some months. The time they were given for the moon was not a gift, and those hours had to be made up somehow, she would explain to her mother when questioned about why she couldn't come home for a long weekend here or there. The gossip and giggles of junior associates, paralegals, and interns meant nothing to her. Let them talk, she told herself. *It's not like they have anything real to say.*

***

That was, until the day she stepped onto the elevator going up to the executive floor. The conversation that was taking place between two other partners immediately halted as she stepped into the car. Ekins was a cat shifter, a senior partner like Grayson, with his name over the door. He was older, a bit more hands-off, and had always treated her respectfully. He nodded, his eyes lowering as the doors slid shut, but it was the other man's reaction that caught her attention. He was younger, only recently named partner in the past six months or so, a salaried position without equity of his own. He had been the one talking, the one who had cut off abruptly. His eyes also lowered, but his mouth held the shadow of a smirk, and she had no doubt that he would resume whatever crass thing he'd been saying the instant she left.

She'd not often been the source of gossip in her lifetime, but Vanessa knew without question that she had been the topic of this man's conversation, at least one half of it. She never turned to the doors, remaining facing the men at the elevator glided upwards, waiting for the younger man to make his mistake. She didn't have to wait long. His eyes lifted from his shoes, catching hers, unable to look away as she stared him down. She knew from the hint of color that reddened his ears that she was not wrong in her assumptions.

Her nose couldn't pick out his scent, but she knew what he wasn't. He wasn't a wolf, was not an apex predator in any situation. He didn't possess the spine of steel they did, the fearlessness and indomitability they did. She wasn't sure what he was, but he may as well have been a human. After a few moments, his chin jutted out, lips curling into a sneer as if he'd only just remembered he was several stations above her in the firm's hierarchy, and Vanessa smiled in response. *I'm going to ruin this man's whole fucking career.*

"Fine weather we're having this week." Her voice was overloud in the small, silent car, ringing with confidence. "Judge Ludstrohm is always in a good mood when the weather is nice. That bodes well for us."

“Any day he can get onto the Ketterling court means fast and easy cases,” Ekins agreed with a chuckle, his eyes raising to give her a warm smile.

They bounced to a soft stop, the doors opening with a ding on the floor beneath Grayson’s office. She didn’t need to feed them more ammunition, she had decided as soon as she’d seen the man’s smirk. She grumbled the entire way she stomped up the stairs, Johanna raising an eyebrow when she burst through the door.

“Johanna, what do you know about that new guy, Brock?”

The older she-wolf’s lips turned up in a pink-painted smile.

“I know his Majesty doesn’t care for him. He’s someone’s brother-in-law, I think? There was something shady with him at his previous firm, poaching clients, something like that. It all got swept under the rug before he was hired. I was surprised when they gave him a partner, but I think Gray just went along with it. He knew he was outvoted.”

"Does he not like him because of poaching clients?" That sort of behavior was unscrupulous, but it was precisely Grayson's MO, she thought.

"No, I believe he said something about not liking how he smells?"

Vanessa snorted, pushing open the door to his office, knowing she would have been stopped had he been in the middle of something. His eyebrow raised as soon as the door closed behind her. "I know that pissy look isn't for me."

"No, it's for that smirky motherfucker you made partner, even though he doesn't have enough chips to buy his way in."

Grayson began to laugh before she'd even finished. "Brock? I fucking hate that asshole. He's a weasel or a badger, some overgrown rodent, I'm positive. The smell of him makes my stomach turn. Why? What did he do? Did he say something to you?"

She was in front of his chair by then, trapped between him and the desk, and she knew the expression on her face couldn't be described as anything other than pouty.

"It's fine, don't worry about it."

"It's not fine if it has you so worked up. Tell me what he did so I can ensure he's punished accordingly."

Vanessa smiled, huffing out an aggrieved breath. "Why does it matter? I'm just a mid-level associate. What I think doesn't matter."

"It matters if I say it matters." He crowded her against the desk, gripping her chin and tilting her face to meet his eye. "And it matters if he upset you. And if you want him punished, he will be. What my baby wants, my baby gets."

She dissolved into giggles against his shirt front. "Oh yeah? Since when? Do you think we might get a break after the holidays? Is there ever a point when things slow down?"

"So we can go to Tahiti?"

"Bora Bora," she corrected. "I don't know what the point in fucking a rich asshole is if he's never going to take me to the *one* place I want to go. Your shoe shine guy would probably be a better sugar daddy."

"Did you come all the way up here to bust my balls for no reason? Did you just want to complain about someone without really complaining? What do you actually need?"

Vanessa pressed her lips together, unwilling to admit that she *had*, in fact, been coming up to his office to engage his balls, only not in the way to which he was alluding. She wanted to lean over his desk, let him slide his cock home, and help her stop squirming in her seat. She'd had the dream again early that morning, had woken with slickness between her thighs and an ache in her core that only he could diminish. Grayson must've sensed her true motivation, smelled it on the air, more likely, as he gave her a shark-like grin. Sure enough, he lowered his nose to the side of her neck, inhaling deeply.

"Mmmm . . . Did you come up here just to make my cock hard, rabbit?" He buried his face in her hair, breathing her in, rubbing the silky strands between his thumb and forefinger, groaning as he did so, keeping her locked in the steel cage of his arms. "You smell good enough to eat." His whisper made the hair stand up on her neck, a shiver down her back. "You're making my balls ache, Vanessa."

She gripped the front of his shirt, needing him desperately, refusing to admit it.

"Tell me what you need, babydoll." He palmed her jaw, his hand engulfing her head, thumb sweeping over the apple of her cheek. Vanessa leaned into the pressure for the space of several heartbeats, wanting nothing more than to melt against him, before snapping herself out of it.

"I don't *need* anything," she insisted peevishly, his sly smile causing her to stiffen. She didn't like admitting that she *needed* him for anything, and certainly not for this.

He'd long been relocated to his executive suite by then, the glass-walled cube in front of her desk empty for several days before a senior associate moved in. The first time she'd stepped off the elevator on the upper floor, she had exclaimed over the frigid temperature, and Johanna had shrugged, tugging her heavy cardigan a bit tighter.

“I’d rather have to bring a sweater every day than listen to him throwing up all afternoon at least once a week. The cold helps with the headaches.”

Vanessa told herself that the cold air was the reason her nipples pebbled beneath her shift dress. It had nothing at all to do with the dream she’d had and the heated state she’d woken in. The restless state she was *still* in, if she were being honest with herself, which she didn’t actually feel like being at that moment. The dream was one she’d had repeatedly, owing to the full moon activities that had taken place the prior month. She disliked having it, for the previous month had been *terrible*. She hated the way he’d made her feel, hated that what they’d done had been the byproduct of their argument, and the fact that it had become a recurring fantasy made her blood boil with more than just arousal.

***

Going to court the week of the moon was unorthodox, and most of the time, opposing counsel worked with them to make arrangements, but that month she'd not been so lucky. She had been on heat suppressants since puberty, but she'd only needed to take the wolfsbane suppressant one other time in her life, in her university days. The pills had a chalky, artificial taste going down, and she'd gagged as she'd swallowed them. Her wolf would be in agony. A different sort of ache lay in store, along with low-grade nausea and an itchiness in her skin, but she would be in court. She would remain in her human skin as the moon reached its zenith, her muscles and bones staying exactly as they were, and she would show up to court as scheduled.

He had been furious.

"I already tried to have it changed. Counsel understands, it's their clients. They're just being dicks because they can. It's fine. I'll get through it."

"It's *not* fine, Vanessa. It's absolutely unacceptable. We're filing an injunction and making a complaint with the bar against this firm."

She listened as he paced and raged, citing every bit of legislation he could argue in her favor, every case that had previously been won, his annoyance redirected at her when she remained steadfast.

"I don't want you getting involved. This is *my* career, Gray. We all have to make sacrifices; we've all made sacrifices before and will have to make them again. This isn't any different."

"I will not accept this. These are not the sort of concessions that should be asked of us, any of us. We shouldn't have to —"

"Maybe *you* haven't. You," she spat in frustration, "but the rest of us normies have to make those sorts of sacrifices. Most people don't have daddy to call to snap his fingers and make everything work out in our favor. This case has nothing to do with you, and I don't want you involved!"

"Vanessa, that's *my* name over the door, not yours. *My* reputation in our community. And I'm not going to tolerate this sort of—"

"I don't want you getting involved!"

Her voice rattled in the corners of the room, rising in volume and pitch until he finally stopped talking. His mouth pressed in a flat line, and his dark eyes narrowed at her until they were little more than black slits in his face. She didn't want to have to make the accommodation, but she didn't want him stepping in for her. She'd already known then they were the source of gossip, and it wouldn't do to fan the flames. *Like he said, his name is over the door. You have nothing except everything to lose.*

"I-I just want to get through this, alright? Don't look at me like that. I'm doing the right thing for our client, and I just need to get through it. I'm still coming over on Tuesday, though?"

He'd turned away from her and took his time answering.

"I can't, I'm sorry. The smell of that garbage you took is making me sick. You should probably go."

She'd felt his words like a slap, stinging against her skin, her mouth hanging open in disbelief. He grimaced, pulling a face as if he'd swallowed something rotten, and she'd felt a tidal wave of rage surging through her, wanting to do nothing more than pick up one of the heavy office chairs and bash him upside his perfect, stupid jaw.

"It tastes like a dirty penny."

"Grayson," she gritted out, furious with herself for being so close to tears, "I hate you sometimes. I hate you *so fucking* much."

She was the one who had to do this; she was the one who would be putting her body through something unnatural. He didn't have to like it, but a smidgen of kindness would be nice from someone who allegedly loved her. *Why would you think that? He's never said it. He's never shown you that he might. You're a monthly diversion, something to stick his dick in. That's it.*

"We have that in common, at least. I hate that you're doing this. So, I suppose we're even, rabbit."

She'd shaken with barely suppressed rage the rest of the week. It was somewhat gratifying when opposing counsel was chastised by the judge for the fact that any of them were there, but she'd not forgotten the source of her anger, returning to her apartment for less than an hour before filling her gas tank and following the GPS directions to the lake. She would be there waiting for him in the morning, would be there waiting to tell him what a fucking asshole he really was, and that she was done. He could find someone new to chase because she was done being his prey, done being his verbal sparring partner, done with him.

Her anger had lent itself to a heavy foot, and she'd arrived at the cabin far earlier than she'd thought the trip would take. Everyone experienced the change differently, and she never remembered what it was like to be an apex predator for a short while every month, but she knew the moment she stopped, walking between her car and the cabin doors, what it was like to be prey.

She could feel the weight of heavy eyes on her, could sense his heat, could hear the heavy panting breaths. It might not even be him, she realized. There were other wolves out that night, other wolves prowling beneath the full moon. Her heart was beating so loud and fast that she was surprised it wasn't causing a shift in the air, palpable friction around her. *Just move slowly. Move slowly to the door, and you'll be fine.* She had barely taken another step when she heard the growl.

She'd always been extremely fast, was light and quick on her feet, and she sprung towards the cabin, clattering up the steps and throwing herself at the locked door. *Locked.* She couldn't remember if he locked the door the previous month, only that they had arrived early enough to put the bed to use, knotting her in his man skin one final time before he had her as a wolf that night, and that she had woken the previous morning in the crook of his arm, her nose against his sternum and his hands in her hair. The keys lived in the same key ring he used for his truck, the sleek luxury sportscar remaining in Bridgeton each month. The keys might well still be in the truck, for she had watched him toss them back in through the open window on more than one occasion; convenient for a fast getaway, he had laughed. The truck was parked away from the cabin, in a cleared-out, paved-over space near the road, and she would need to get there.

It was a straight line from where she currently cowered on the cabin's front porch, and she'd already run from whoever was there in the trees once. They would overtake her quickly, now that she was coming from the staircase, without the cover of her car. Vanessa gathered herself, steeling her nerves. It might be Grayson, but it could be anyone. She took a running leap off the porch, over the steps, sliding in the gravel for the space of a heartbeat before she was off, around the other side of the cabin, moving toward the lake.

In a matter of seconds, the beast was in pursuit. Her heart climbed into her lungs, making it even more difficult to suck in a breath as she raced forward. The wet smell of the lake rose around her, muddy and green, and she careened around the back of the house, nearly losing her footing in the damp grass. She could smell him behind her, could hear him in pursuit, gnashing teeth and hot breath, and she wondered if he could smell her fear. All around her, the sounds of the forest at night had gone silent — the crickets were holding their breath, tree frogs gone mute, the belching bullfrogs in the water vanished. Nothing existed except for the gathering growl behind her and the sound of his loping pace, not even needing to run in his pursuit.

She had just crossed the small mound leading to the dock when she made her fatal mistake. Meaning to zig when she ought to have zagged, she was tackled in the grass. Her body rolled, feeling the squish of mud between her fingers, a rock beneath her lower back, and then the press of a massive body over hers, hooked claws grazing her skin as her wrists were forced above her head.

The smell hit her nose, and she whimpered, arousal flooding her core, for, of course, it was him. She would know his scent anywhere and would never be able to smell anyone else ever again, but she didn't know if he would be able to smell *her* through the wolfsbane. He was huge and hulking, pitch black with shining eyes that reflected the moonlight and teeth she could have seen ten paces away, teeth that were currently snapping at her neck.

"Grayson . . ."

The first bump of his cold, wet nose against her skin made her gasp, teeth glancing off her skin as he nipped at her arm, at her shoulder, at her hair. She hadn't realized she was crying until a rough tongue swiped over her cheeks. Inside, her wolf was screaming. *It wasn't right!* It was unnatural to be bound in her bones this way, and her wolf writhed, wanting to run with him, where she belonged. Her thin T-shirt dress was shredded from her body, and he snapped at her throat, hot tongue trailing down her bare, white skin.

When his muzzle pushed between her legs, she gasped, gripping the thick, black fur at his shoulders. A growl gathered in his throat, concealed behind the supple black fur, sleek to her touch. *Even his wolf is like a perfectly groomed show dog.* He inhaled against her stomach, against her inner thighs, pushing his nose against the lips of her sex and breathing her in, snarling in rage when the smell of her ended, and the suppressant began.

She arched beneath him, her wolf howling in agony and frustration, and for a moment, Vanessa thought her spine might pop. It desperately wanted to lengthen and curve, to transform into something primal and powerful, wanted to be with him in the way they were meant to be together and not trapped this way. His hooked, silver-tipped claws dug into the dirt on either side of her head, raking and slicing at the earth instead of her flesh, because he knew her. Knew her scent, knew her wolf, and if he had dug his claws into her flesh, ripping her open, searching for her wolf, she wouldn't have blamed him. They were scent mates, and she couldn't deny it any longer—puzzle pieces that were only whole when they were fitted together, and it didn't matter if he didn't love her or if there were other women; didn't matter what she did with other men. They were only whole together, and she would do whatever she needed to keep him chasing her forever.

The first pass of his rough tongue made her suck in a shuddering breath, while the third made her cry out. Her voice echoed through the black woods, a moan that was nearly a sob as his rough tongue licked over her clit, again and again, pressing into her opening and growling against her heat. There was nothing unnatural about the situation, she decided, for she belonged there with him. The only unnatural thing was her, the drugs in her system and the agony beneath her skin. She knew he would be able to taste them on her, but perhaps his wolf knew he had pushed her a touch too far. After all, what would he have to chase if she stopped leading him?

She still felt the burn beneath her skin and the pressure on her spine where her wolf wanted to burst free, but he still knew exactly how to lick her clit, even in this form. She gripped the black fur at his neck, thrusting upwards against the wolfish snout, riding his face as she had countless times before, not stopping until she gushed on his tongue.

His cock in this form looked nothing like his own. Thick and red, rising from a short, black-skinned sheath, he was already dripping. He had pushed up on his knees after coating his mouth in her release, muzzle shining in the moonlight, and his cock loomed over her. She needed to turn over, needed to get on her knees for him, but she wanted to touch him first. Her nail traced a snaking vein from base to tip, her thumb rolling over the slightly pointed tip, gripping his shaft as best she could as his dark red knot swelled at the bottom of his shaft.

When he mounted her, she did nothing to stop him. Held her ass up high, as she would have done in her other skin. The air left her body when the tip of his head caught at her lips, breaching her for the first time. He already had the biggest cock she'd ever ridden in his everyday form; his wolf's was bigger. His wolf's was bigger, but she was not, her pathetic human body struggling to accommodate his stretch. Vanessa's eyes rolled back when he began to thrust, every drag of him within her seeming to displace one of her vertebrae. She laced her small, white fingers with his, huge and black and claw-tipped, moaning again when she felt the press of his knot at her entrance. Her anger, at least for the moment, was forgotten, and she hoped this meant his was as well.

"Knot me, baby," she whined, gasping as he snarled against her. His pace was relentless and driving, and she pushed back against him. "I want to take your knot, Gray. It belongs to me. *You* belong to *me*."

She felt she was being cleaved in two, each rock of his hips making her jolt, her head lolling. His teeth snapped at her neck, and his hips surged, and the world went white in an explosion of pain and bliss, his knot sealing them together. She shook beneath him, her climax tinged with pain, pleasure and pain, and she felt his teeth at her shoulder again as the pressure within her continued to increase. She realized he was filling her womb, her a flood of molten heat that made her belly bulge, a growl ripping from his throat as he emptied within her.

She had leaked the evidence of their coupling for several days, necessitating the use of a panty liner for the first time in ages. Since then, the dream of being taken by his wolf in her human form had been a regular fantasy. She *hated* that it got her so wet, hated that it made her so needy, for it was mortifying to contemplate, positively embarrassing to admit, and worst of all—he had been a smug shit about it, even more puffed up than he usually was, in danger of floating away.

***

"Are you dreaming of my wolf again?" he asked with a sly smile, crowding her against his desk.

"No," she insisted indignantly, knowing he could tell she was lying. He backed her up until her ass hit the edge of the desk, not stopping until he'd lifted her onto it with a squeak.

"I think we both know that's not true, rabbit. Why don't you let me give you what you need."

It was one thing to share his bed each month in the lead-up to the moon. It was quite a different matter for him to sit before her in his giant leather chair, rolling to the desk and lifting her legs around him, easing up her skirt until he could lower his head and nip her thighs.

"Don't tell me this isn't what you want. You're already dripping for me."

His nose pressed to the front of her panties, pressing into her slickness. A deep, rumbling groan vibrated against her skin, and she sighed in spite of herself, her legs dropping open a bit further for him. "That's it, baby. Let me take care of you."

His first lick was against the pink silk, hot and wet and exactly the way she remembered his wolf's tongue feeling that night. She truly *did* feel guilty for being so terrible at sucking his cock, Vanessa thought, breath shuddering out of her, for he could teach a master class in eating her out. He hummed against her skin in appreciation, thick tongue sliding into her folds, his lips fastening on her like the suction end of a tentacle. He sucked and licked, bumping her with his nose, providing slurping kisses to her clit that made her toes curl, acting like a man starved and not one who'd had an eighty-dollar steak for lunch.

Vanessa gripped his hair, rocking her pelvis into him with small gasps, too conscious of his assistant right outside the locked door. He pulled back slightly, and she tightened her grip on his hair, worried that he was about to torture her with stopping, but he'd only been moving his hand into place, two thick fingers sliding into her as his lips re-fastened on her clit. Her climax started behind her navel, heat building and spreading until her knees were shaking, stretched around his mountain-like shoulders. The addition of his fingers sent her over the edge, and she rode his tongue to a spine-quivering release, white sparks shooting behind her eyes as she gripped his hair and tried to hold in her moan of pleasure.

She was sheepish when she looked down at him, a self-satisfied grin splitting his face, glistening with her release.

"Do you need to . . ."

"Yeah," he agreed, sucking his fingers clean. "I do."

Her hands worked nimbly at his belt buckle when he stood, reaching in and drawing out his stiffened length, already thick and straining. When he pushed his fat cockhead into her, she expected him to hilt himself until he was balls deep. That was how he liked fucking her, as deep as he could go, his pelvis flush to hers, but he didn't. Back and forth several times, just the head, breaching her over and over again. Holding himself in hand, he slid his cock tip up and down her folds, from cunt to clit, coating himself in her slick. She reached down to cup his balls, full and fat in her hand, rolling and squeezing, helping him along as he began to penetrate her shallowly once more.

"You need to get back to work, rabbit. You have those depositions to get through."

His face flushed red with the force of swallowing down his groan, the first spurt of white creaming against her clit, quickly followed by several more of varying volume. He would've been throwing ropes across her body had he been standing upright, but with his slit pressed to her folds, his ejaculation was a long, voluminous ooze of sticky white cream. When he kissed her gently, pulling her panties up and trapping his semen against her, she nearly fell off the desk.

"Go back to work. Don't forget who this pussy belongs to."

She should have gone directly to the bathroom and wiped herself clean, but instead, Vanessa found herself getting back in the elevator. When she stepped out on her floor, her cheeks were pink. She wondered if anyone would look at her and know that her panties were full, if they would be able to smell him on her. If they were a wolf, it was possible. She was afraid to sit down and ruin her dress, and she puttered around her desk, reading as much as she could while standing until the mess he'd created had cooled into an uncomfortable presence, forcing her to teeter into the restroom, wiping herself clean of him, at least for the moment.

* * *

Chapter Eleven

4 Months Earlier . . .

"What will happen if someone finds out about us?"

They were in his bed, at his house in Cambric Creek, her favorite place to be.

She hadn't expected to reacclimate to suburbia as well as she had, but Cambric Creek was an intriguing little town. There were plenty of exclusive little boutiques and high-end bistros, all of which knew his dietary restrictions on sight. Three of them even stocked his favorite champagne. She'd had her hair done at the same chichi salon his mother and sister-in-law patronized, marveling at the volumizing treatment and the peach stone facial she'd received.

"I've offered to give you an all-natural facial numerous times," he'd huffed as she continued to go on about it that evening, rubbing the back of his hand against her cheek to feel how smooth her skin was.

She loved laying out on one of the deck chairs in his resort-like backyard, removing her bikini top to sunbathe, feeling the weight of his eyes watching her from the upper deck. She would stretch like a cat, rising slowly once the sun was too hot on her skin, diving into the pool in one long glide and finding him waiting for her when she emerged, her bikini bottoms joining the top, abandoned on the deck.

She liked the quiet darkness of the big rooms, finding it easy to think and turn her mind off, putting work aside, at least in tiny increments. Nothing was more relaxing than sitting against the sofa in his big, empty living room, sipping from a mug of tea as the rain spattered against the wall of windows. She hadn't grown up in a big house and scarcely knew what to do with so much space, but Vanessa would be hard-pressed to say that she didn't like it.

The master bedroom was nearly as big as her entire apartment in Bridgeton, his bed a sumptuous oasis of high-thread-count Egyptian cotton and feather-stuffed pillows, and some mornings, waking up beside him after working off the edge of her muted pre-moon heat, she thought it would be nice to never have to leave again. That evening, however, her mind was not as relaxed.

She couldn't get the incident with the elevator out of her head. She'd begun to feel paranoid in the following weeks, assuming she was being whispered about whenever her back was turned, and it had started to affect her performance with her team.

"If the partners know, that means everyone knows. The top office is always the last to find out about anything. That means people have been talking about us for months! Everyone probably already knows . . . What am I going to do?!"

He said nothing in response, and after several yawning moments of silence, Vanessa huffed, lifting her head from his chest to glare up at him.

"I'm not ignoring you. I'm not sure what question I'm being asked. So people find out? Who the fuck cares? Has anything ever impacted our work? No. They're always going to look for something to whisper about. What's going to happen? Nothing."

She frowned at his answer but wasn't sure what she had been expecting. His eyes closed, satisfied that the issue was closed, and after a few minutes, the steady rise and fall of his chest told her he was hovering just on the edge of sleep, and she should have kept her thoughts to herself.

"I don't know if that's true."

His eyes fluttered open, his eyes narrowing in her direction.

"What do you think would happen, rabbit? What would happen realistically? Neither of us is married. I'm not even your direct supervisor, not technically. I'll be reprimanded by Vormir for not disclosing, and that would be it."

Her stomach twisted, knowing he wasn't thinking things through thoroughly and wasn't seeing things from her end. She didn't want her career hamstrung because of their relationship, not when he would walk away without repercussion, by his own admission. Her reputation would be irreparably tarnished. *Sleeping with the boss, sleeping her way to the top, special treatment that she didn't deserve, special positioning on cases, about as useful as a first-year law student.*

"Nothing will happen to *you*, Gray."

He was quiet again, and she thought he had probably decided to ignore her and her silly fears and go to sleep. He had nothing to worry about, for his name was over the door, and there would be no legacy of whispers that would trail after him, from courtroom to courtroom for the rest of his legal career.

"We can file a declaration with HR on Monday, Vanessa. Would that make you feel better? I really don't know what else you want me to do. And you understand that filing with HR is basically filing to me, right? We're making a declaration to the company, agreeing not to sue the company. You're essentially agreeing that you will not sue *me* over me, and the rest of the partners will be made aware. That's about the only official recourse there is, but if that's what you want to do, that's what we'll do."

She didn't know why she'd asked the question, didn't know what answer she had gone poking for, but that hadn't been it. Filing a declaration with HR would make things *official*, official in the eyes of their coworkers, official together. *And then what?* The insidious little voice in her head asked. *Caught. You're not going to smell like prey for very long, rabbit, not unless you keep running. He's going to get bored. He's going to find someone new to chase, something more exciting than what he has waiting at home.*

They spent every moon together, the smell of him sending her heat into overdrive until he calmed the fire in her blood. She joined his family for brunch, sat amongst Owen's equally reserved girlfriend and Trapp's human schoolteacher, cooed appropriately over Jackson's precocious little boy, had laughed with his mother, and parlayed with his father.

When she'd told him about her cousin's out-of-town wedding, a cousin with whom she'd always been competitive, she was shocked when he'd agreed before she fully had the question out.

"Of course," he'd said seriously, leaning forward across the table, his dark brows drawn together, "family is important." In the course of the weekend trip, he'd somehow managed to convince her family that she was the most brilliant legal mind in the city, had impressed her relatives and made her mother blush like a teenager, made her sparkle at his side until her mother had asked where she'd been hiding him and why on earth hadn't she sealed the deal yet.

She attempted to take care of him, as much as he would let her when an aura hit without warning, and there was no place safer in the world than curled to his chest, wrapped in his arms. She wasn't quite sure how they'd gotten there, but it very nearly felt like a real, stable relationship, a notion that worried her as much as it thrilled. She loved having Grayson Hemming chase her, didn't ever want him to *stop* chasing her, and she didn't want him to start thinking of their time together as an entrapment. She tilted her head up, pressing a kiss to the base of his neck.

"You're right. I don't think that's necessary. It seems silly to get HR involved in our private business. Like you said, the other partners have to be notified. It might make things awkward. We don't have that sort of relationship, so there's no need to blow it up into something it's not. I just want to ensure we're not doing anything stupid that will impact either of us down the road. I hate knowing people are whispering every time I walk into the room, but they'll get bored eventually and move on to the next juicy bit of gossip."

He said nothing for a long time, and she thought that perhaps he'd fallen asleep after all. She closed her eyes, rubbing her cheek against his chest, inhaling deeply. Somewhere along the line, he had started smelling like home. When it rumbled out of the darkness, his voice startled her, and her eyes popped open.

"I suppose that's one point of view."

He didn't say anything further, and Vanessa forced her eyes shut, the insidious voice in her head receding, leaving behind the certainty that she had made a terrible misstep.

***

In the end, he boiled their relationship down to fifteen minutes, and she had no one but herself to blame. Fifteen-minute blocks of time, the way he organized his schedule; tiny hash marks that kept him on track, and she — *they* — had been allotted one little square.

She hadn't realized anything was wrong. Work was out of control, consuming every waking minute of the day and the hours she was meant to be sleeping. One of the firm's minor clients — one of *her* clients — had taken their IPO public, becoming an overnight millionaire, and suddenly a handful of the people above her, senior associates and partners included, wanted to edge their way in, insisting the account needed tighter stewardship.

Her client, a young wolf in her twenties who had founded her own makeup line, had kiboshed their efforts. She didn't want to deal with anyone except Vanessa and especially didn't want *that* guy — pointing her long, manicured nail at Brock, who'd somehow slipped into the meeting —anywhere near her, said with her nose wrinkling, winking at Vanessa once her back had turned. Grayson had remained blissfully absent for the entire debacle, and she'd handled it on her own. He had been absent for much of the month, she'd realized more than two weeks into it, shrugging it off, buoyed by her independent success. It might have seemed odd to outsiders, but he was in court constantly, and she was engaged in the big law race of billable hours, chained to her desk for much of the week. *He's as busy as you are, probably in court.*

Her first clue should have been the apartment. He was having work done at the house, he'd muttered, and they'd spent their first full moon in Bridgeton in she couldn't remember how long. She realized long after the fact that the work being done was a professional deep cleaning — every surface sanitized and steamed, the carpets and bedding and curtains, all of it — shampooed, disinfected, rugs beaten and washed, the contents of the linen closet and bathroom closet emptied and cleaned, leaving behind an empty sterility, devoid of her smell.

Not spending the day with his family after the moon had felt strange, but when he'd remained distracted and out-of-sorts, she'd begged off dinner, going back to her own apartment to catch up on some much-needed sleep, not realizing she should have been clinging to every moment, paying attention to his oddly somber, un-Grayson-like mood.

The schedule tap had appeared on her laptop calendar a week later, an hour or so after she'd first arrived at her desk, a fifteen-minute time slot. It was that fact that stuck in her throat for days and weeks afterward, keeping her company in the bath and in her empty bed.

She had been there for six years, three of them with him. They had somehow managed to balance their working relationship and personal life together for three years, and it was only in the last five months that her co-workers had taken notice, an impressive feat, quite frankly.

"I wanted you to hear it from me. I'm speaking with all of the senior associates today, and an email will be going out to the staff later, but . . . I wanted you to hear it directly from me. Effective this afternoon, I'm no longer affiliated with this firm. My clients have already been redistributed, and I'm not taking any of them with me, so you don't need to worry about any of your caseloads dropping. You'll be running second on Hastings–Durning. Ekins will be overseeing, but you've always had a good relationship with him, so I don't foresee there being any issue."

It was a practiced speech, one he'd probably already given a dozen times in part and would do a dozen more times that day. Not one for a girlfriend or lover or whatever the hell she was.

"Did-did they fire you?! They couldn't have, not without a vote! But-but your stake —"

"We've agreed to a buyout of my stake in the company."

She reeled, unable to fully process his words. There was no way she would come in tomorrow and Grayson not be there, terrorizing some junior associate. She had to be dreaming.

"So what, you're just . . . leaving? Retiring? You're forty years old; what are you going to do, take up gardening?"

"I'm not retiring," he scoffed. "Effective first of next month, I'll be chief internal counsel for the Werewolf Defense League. I'll be transitioning into my role there in the interim."

Vanessa sat back in her seat. She felt winded, as if she had just run up a steep staircase, racing away from a great beast nipping at her heels.

"You think you'll be happy doing non-profit? What happened to having expensive tastes?"

"It's the right thing to do. And I'm employed by the agency. It's not like I'm volunteering my time. My equity in the firm is being bought out, and I've been offered a generous compensation package for my clients. I *could* retire now if I wanted to. Financial has had plenty of time to hammer things out."

She wanted to point out the vast difference between being a salaried employee for a non-profit agency and being the co-owner of a multi-million dollar firm, but his words froze her. She realized then that this had been a deal long in the works. And he had never told her.

"How long? How long, Gray?"

"I don't know what you—"

"How long, Grayson?" Her voice was sharp, a mortifying waver over his name, her emotions closer to the surface than she'd thought. She realized, as soon as the words were out, that she already knew.

His head cocked, the same look he'd given her that night in his glass cube, when she'd offered to fuck him.

"A month? Maybe a month and a half?"

She realized the magnitude of her folly, that night in bed. Instead of marching into HR to make an official declaration of their relationship, he'd gone marching into the managing partner's office to quit. He'd never let on that her words had hurt him, that he felt differently, that they *did* have exactly *that sort of relationship*. Just a stone poker face, distance these last six weeks, and now this. An exit from their shared professional life without discussion or preamble.

"I can't believe you're doing this."

"Isn't this what you wanted," he answered sharply, the first spark of actual emotion he'd displayed since she'd entered the office. "Give it a week, maybe two. No one will bat an eyelash when you walk into the room."

"I only meant that I don't want—"

"I don't have that luxury, Vanessa. People are going to talk no matter where I go, whether here, this new place, or the fucking grocery store. I don't care about whispers. Whoever I'm with can't care about them either . . . and now you won't have to. And if someone wants to start something with you, you can tell them the truth. We don't have that sort of relationship."

An exit from their shared professional life and apparently their personal life as well, she realized. His words felt like a physical blow, and she wanted to hunch against the pain. The small timer on his computer calendar dinged, an indication she had run down the clock on her allotted fifteen minutes, running down the clock on their relationship without even realizing it. The parroting back of her words spoke volumes, she thought; told of how long he'd been chewing on them and the way they'd evidently set into his heart like a blade, one she'd unwittingly cast. *I only meant to keep you chasing.*

She barely remembered drifting back to her desk, drifting through the rest of the day, the rest of the week, the rest of the month. She remembered the anger she felt several days later, once the shock had faded. They'd begun their relationship on a joint decision, but he'd completely left her out of the negotiations on its ending, and she wasn't quite sure she could forgive him that. The first full moon without him was an agony, and she couldn't forgive him that either. He'd done this to spite her rather than talking through his emotions and what he wanted. She ignored that she was just as culpable in that regard. After all, she had been playing games from the moment he'd taken up residence in the fishbowl office.

Most aggravatingly, he was right — the whispers had faded after that second week of his absence, at least until he'd gone on vacation. The social media profile was being shared around the junior associates, the information shared with her by the sweet goblin woman who cleaned the offices on her floor. She managed to put it out of her mind the rest of the day, ignoring the renewed giggles that followed her exit from the common rooms, waiting until she was secure in her own apartment.

He didn't have public social media accounts, but somehow this girl's, this stranger's DreameStream photo reel had become public knowledge, and she realized he'd done that to spite her as well. She'd expected someone half his age, a blonde with big tits and no gag reflex, like the one who'd sucked him off at the Lupercalia party, but instead, the young woman who smiled up from the photograph was maybe a handful of years younger than herself. She was petite and small-boned, with dark hair and eyes, and the knowledge that he'd taken someone on vacation — someone who looked like her, to the same sort of tropical locale she'd wanted to visit with him — had broken something in her brain.

The scream that had ripped from her throat had been primal in nature. She screamed and raged, and her wolf screamed along with her. She flipped her coffee table, flung a book at the mirror in the hallway, had felt as if she might spontaneously turn, her wolf shifting in her bones and wreaking havoc on everything in her path. She wanted to shred his skin with her nails, castrate him with her bare hands, and make him pay with blood for every sharp word and insult to her work, for mixed signals and hypocrisy, for having the audacity to introduce her to his family and make her feel welcome, to give her a glimpse of what a life together might look like . . . She wanted to make him realize how *miserable* he would be without her. She was humiliated, was beyond furious, *hated* him . . . and she loved hating him, she realized. She loved hating him, and she *hated* how much she loved him.

***

With the destruction had come clarity.

She was not giving up that easily, and if that was what he wanted, he could go fuck himself. *She* led *him*, not the other way around. He had said she was a talented litigator, and she knew more about him than anyone outside his immediate family. *His family.* His family was where her play was, what her strategy would be routed around. He was driven by a single purpose — to be better than his brother, in all things, in every way. A war for their father's attention they'd begun fighting in infancy and a futile one at that, because it seemed exceedingly apparent to her that Jack Hemming was most delighted by his three eldest sons as a collective.

Family was his weakness. Jackson made him act irrationally and his father could convince him to do something like leave his lucrative career to come work for one of his pet charities. She had watched his father make his sons dance like puppets, and she would do the same. She loved having Grayson Hemming chase her, and despite this grievous misstep, despite his childish temper tantrum, Vanessa knew she could make him chase her again.

She was familiar, of course, with the WDL. She had passed whatever unspoken test his father had set for her — her werewolf pedigree, her early career history as a public defender, focusing on werewolves and shifters — and she'd gone the extra mile, earning extra credit, like the kiss-ass she'd always been, ensuring that the pro bono cases she had worked on to fulfill her bar requirement had been for the Werewolf Defense League, an organization with which he had close ties.

"It's a shame you left public practice," he'd mused, voicing the opposite of the first conversation she'd had with his wife. "The WDL could use someone like you."

"Oh, I don't know about that," she had laughed, ducking her head in an appropriately bashful fashion. "Organizations like that need heavy hitters. I wouldn't be qualified to do much more than filling the coffee machine."

His smile was glinting and sharp, another thing Grayson had inherited.

"Gray said you're brilliant. Passionate and driven, those were his words. Are you calling my son a liar?"

She gave him her best earnest-before-the-judge smile in return, gratified to note that Jackson's wife was sitting close enough to the mouth of the room to observe their conversation.

"Let's see," she mused. "A philanderer. A snob. Entirely too pleased with himself, and a world-class prick. But he's definitely not a liar."

His father's laughter was a smooth roll, his sharp canines glinting in the sunlight pouring in to the room's glass walls. She knew she ought not to feel a little thrill of victory every time she said or did something to make Jack Hemming smile at her, *specifically* at her, which she had learned was very different from his normal generic surface-level smile, but it couldn't be helped. Vanessa wasn't sure how she'd managed it, but she had somehow carved out her own private audience timeslot sitting before the haughty patriarch each week, joining the rotation of his sons.

It wasn't something his daughter-in-law was afforded, not that she seemed to want it. She didn't know if Jackson's wife, Victoria, had cottoned on to the game; she didn't think so. The woman had instead devoted herself to being a pillar of the community and having a good relationship with her mother-in-law, and although Vanessa liked Grayson's mother enormously, Sandi Hemming didn't have any of her sons jumping through hoops of fire based entirely on her whims. He was haughty and manipulative, but she had very quickly discovered his was the only opinion that seemed to matter in the entire town. Excellent news for her, as he found her interesting and intelligent, and very good for his son.

"Will you keep an ear to the ground for me? I'll be picking up some pro bono work later this year, and I would like to do something for the right cause. If something crops up where I would be useful, please send it my way."

He had done so, and she was forced to admit that she had genuinely enjoyed the work she had done for the organization. It had given her a moment of serious pause, wondering if she would be happier working for an organization like the WDL instead of being a corporate cog in big law. She had noodled over the possibility before returning to the office after her pro bono sabbatical, but once she was back, she was quickly swept up in the day-to day-grind, and the notion was quickly forgotten.

She'd been surprised to learn that they were well acquainted with Grayson, that he had started a bi-monthly drop-in clinic for werewolves in need of legal advice and unable to afford representation, and that he had been volunteering his services to the organization since he was in law school. She had beamed in pride at the time, realizing that the news wasn't actually that shocking. After all, anything Jackson did, Grayson did bigger. Jack Hemming was not at all enthusiastic about carrying on the mantle of tradition expected of his name, but he did believe in service to the community, particularly the werewolf community, and each of his sons had done their part over the years. Jackson did similar work with the WDL, offering quarterly financial planning workshops and budgeting advice for struggling families and those escaping packs. Learning that Grayson had outdone his brother's contribution was the least surprising thing in the world, and for the last year and a half, she had gone with him, spending two days every other month offering legal advice to young women nearly half her age, holding the hands of toddlers and carrying newborns, attempting to emancipate themselves from their packs before their children got any older.

The following month, she'd shown up at the WDL branch for the drop-in clinic, just as she would have if they'd driven together, as they had countless times before. She'd not been surprised by Grayson's absence —he had more important things to address in the main office now, so instead, she'd taken advantage of the new faces and learned all she could about his father's involvement with the organization.

There was another group, she discovered, with which the family was more directly involved. A halfway house, the historic Hemming family home having been donated to the cause the instant Jack had been left control of it. The following month, as she was given the tour of the historic mansion in Cambric Creek's Oldetowne neighborhood as a new volunteer, she'd felt the weight of eyes on her, the man himself standing in the second landing, his wide mouth turned in a knowing smirk.

"We've missed seeing you," he told her sincerely, once they'd reached the second floor and the volunteer coordinator realized she was being momentarily dismissed. "I hope you've not been working too hard."

She wondered what he'd told his parents, if he'd told them anything.

"It's always crazy, you know how that goes. I keep energy bars in my desk and cross my fingers they won't be dinner every night. I only just found out about this group. I didn't realize your family was affiliated with this organization as well. I-I thought it would be smart to find someplace new to do my pro bono fulfillment now that . . . well, now that things are the way they are."

He knew she was lying; she could tell without question. He knew she was lying, and more than that — he knew that *she* knew he could see through her words. His lips turned up again, nodding, agreeing to keep the charade in place.

"This group already existed, but they weren't terribly well-funded, not like the WDL. *They* have national funding. This is . . . it's become a bit of a pet project of mine."

The house was able to support fifteen residents at a time. Young women mostly, some traveling with small children, who had fled their lives in search of new ones, and the house provided them a safe haven to gather their bearings and get on their feet, with the aid of twenty-four-hour security and an undisclosed address.

"It's very admirable work, Jack." She hoped he heard the sincerity in her voice. She was of the quiet opinion that nearly everything wrong with the wolf she loved was the direct fault of the wolf in front of her, but he was charismatic as hell, and she'd always had a competency kink.

"Grayson's mother is from a pack. Did he ever tell you that?"

His unexpected words brought her up short.

"No, he-he hadn't." *People remake themselves all the time.* She was reminded of that conversation in his fish-bowl office over the pens. *You're never better or worse than the person you are each day.* She wondered if that was what he was trying to do, remake himself into a new version of himself, one who'd never known her.

"I suspected not; none of them ever want to mention it. Always too worried about besmirching her honor. She wasn't permitted to work off her pack grounds, wasn't able to go to school. When we met, she was already engaged. She hasn't seen or spoken to her family since the night she left with me. I don't have anything against arranged marriages, plenty of cultures use them, both human and non-human, but that's not what's happening in these packs."

"It's trafficking," she agreed. "They're moving underage girls across state lines for the express purpose of being pack breeders."

"We have a fourteen-year-old arriving today. That's the only reason we're here; the director wanted to review the plan one final time. She was meant to leave this week to go to her new pack and meet the man she was marrying. Instead, her mother put her on a bus with a backpack of food and a number on our volunteer network. Goodbye and good luck. We're not set up for minors, and I fear the state will need to be involved. Gray is currently losing his mind over this, keeps reminding me he's a civil litigator, not a criminal attorney, which he insists I'm going to need if we let her step over the threshold. It's a shame there's no one at home to calm him down."

A flush moved up her neck. She imagined the tight set of his shoulders, could almost hear the hard bark of his courtroom voice, the same one he used in the office when things were down to the wire. She knew adrenaline would keep him going until this issue was settled and his father and the organization were out of hot water, and the resultant brain chemical crash would likely land him in the hospital for an overnight stay.

"We'll see about that."

Jack Hemming graced her with a brilliant, ethereal smile, and Vanessa thought she probably would have been willing to leave her entire family for him as well.

"Of course. Well, I should let you get back to your tour . . . I have a soft spot for fighters, Vanessa. Good luck with your work here."

***

She didn't know how his father conveyed the casual news that he'd seen her, but she knew that if they all claimed their younger brother Lowell was malicious and spiteful, he'd picked up the traits honestly. She could almost hear Grayson's annoyance in the text he'd sent her, and then he was asking her to dinner.

She decided to let him direct her plan of attack, using his own courtroom methodology — they directed the ships, not the wind and current. When he'd arrived late, giving her that familiar cutting smile, she'd known he'd come with his court game face and adjusted her plan accordingly, keeping things light and superficial, ignoring his tan.

"My brother mentioned he saw you last week."

"Your brother?" She looked up sharply from her salad, eyebrows drawing together.

"Jackson. Said you were at the foundation house. I was treated to a fifteen-minute duet between him and my father on what good work the staff does there and how excited they are to have you providing education to the residents."

That's the only reason we're here, the director wanted to go over the plan one final time. She realized Jackson must have been there with his father; was likely still in the office when she and Jack had their little tête-à-tête. *Perfect.*

"He's on the board of directors there, did you know that? So you might be seeing him fairly often if you're planning on transferring your pro bono time to the foundation." His brow was tight and his voice was clipped, biting against the current of her being connected to his brother in any way, forgetting that he directed boats.

"That's nice to hear," she smiled. "I'll be glad to see a familiar face occasionally when I'm there." She watched as his jaw clenched and his hand tightened around his wine glass. "How are you settling in? Easy transition?"

She expected him to bluster. She was well acquainted with his courtroom confidence and thoughtless self-assurance. He believed himself to be the smartest person in the room in any place he occupied. She was not expecting him to deflate visibly before her eyes. His shoulders slumped a fraction, the hard breath he blew out seeming to take his swagger with it.

"I'm so tired," he admitted with a weary laugh. "I haven't been this fucking tired since—"

"Since before you were a partner in your own firm, sitting in your big air-conditioned office with an army of underlings to do the heavy lifting."

She watched him pick up the rocks glass beside his water goblet, swirling the contents before draining it with a chuckle.

"Yeah, that sums it up."

Vanessa swallowed, preparing her thoughts before opening her mouth, but Grayson continued with more unexpected confidences.

"Someone from the national board came in this week. Do you know what they had the audacity to say to me? It was one of those 'tell me I got this job I didn't really want in the first place because of nepotism without telling me' conversations. He said it was too bad I didn't have more experience in public practice; that's what my predecessor came on board with. A shame I hadn't worked in the DA's office before, or — wait for it — that I didn't have any experience as a public defender."

Her laughter was unrestrained, chiming like a bell across the dining room, and the troll at the table beside them turned his head with a cocked eyebrow in her direction.

"Too bad you don't have any of that worthless first-year law student experience," she tittered before another wave of laughter overtook her. "I hope you reminded them that public defenders don't have experience litigating federal trials."

"Oh, that's exactly what I reminded him. Also, my predecessor left because of burnout, yet his hours in court last year were half of mine."

"It's a shame you don't have someone at home with that worthless PD experience with whom you could share attorney-to-attorney privilege."

His eyes met hers for the first time, and Vanessa swallowed, unable to define the emotion she saw there. She had an appointment to get her hair done at the Cambric Creek salon the following week, scheduled to overlap with his mother's and sister-in-law's, the next plan of her attack, and seeing him like this — looking vaguely miserable — made her swallow down the impulse to push her way onto his lap, wrapping her arms around his neck until he called her rabbit and babydoll and forgot about the last few months entirely.

Playing games is what got you into this mess in the first place, the little voice in her head whispered.

"How did we get here, Gray? I still don't even know how we got here. How am I supposed to know what you want when we've *never* talked about things? *You* don't even know what the fuck you want! You completely changed careers out of the blue, to spite me and make your dad happy. But guess what? You spiting me has made your dad a little less happy with you, and now it sounds like you might hate your job. So who's winning? Who gets to be the victor in this one, counselor? I didn't mean to hurt you, Grayson, but everything you've done since then has been very deliberately designed to hurt me."

He said nothing for a long moment, his eyes raising from the tablecloth to glance around the room.

"Actually, I know exactly what I want right now. Another drink."

She let out the breath she hadn't realized she'd been holding, her confidence that she could fix things shriveling. *What's gone is gone. Too late to try and set parame-*

ters around things now. She jumped when he hooked her pinky with his own across the table, biting her lip as the obsequious server appeared to whisk away the empty rocks glass, reappearing shortly after with a fresh drink.

"Since when do you drink anything other than champagne?"

"I'm contemplating taking up alcoholism, actually. It seems like the next logical step to achieving a triumvirate of poor decisions. Someone asked me if I was planning on doing gardening, but I don't think my cuticles would take well to the dirt. A hobby is a hobby, though, right?"

Her shoulders shook in laughter as she laced their fingers fully, swallowing down the tears that burned at the corner of her eyes.

"Please don't. You already have a terrible personality, sober. And I don't think your poor brain could handle that. It's not too late to walk back on some of those poor decisions, you know. It *should* be, but it's not. Well . . . actually, Shrike has your office now. I don't think you can walk back on *that* one. Are you even going to have time to plan your party this year?"

"That's what event planners are for. I'll be lucky if I can even get the night off. What about you, rabbit? Are you going to be ready to run?"

Her heart thrilled, hearing her pet name for the first time in what felt like an eternity, but for all her talk, she didn't know what she wanted either. She *was* ready to run, was *always* ready to run, wanted him to keep chasing her forever. She wouldn't know what to do with herself if she were caught, but it was looking more and more likely like she either needed to face the snare or find a new running partner.

"Of course," she agreed with a wide smile. "If I have a party to go to, that is. I wonder who might catch me this year, it's a wide-open field." She held his eye as she drained her own glass, wondering if he would even care to claim her. Vanessa realized, for the first time, how exhausting this all was. She was chasing him, for the first time in their relationship, and she fucking hated it.

"And you know what they say. After the ceremony, the chase is the fun part."

* * *

The Capture

Chapter Twelve

Lupercalia

"I didn't expect to see you here tonight."

Vanessa turned at the familiar deep voice, his scent catching her nose, similar to Grayson but just different enough. Not as icy cool, peppery at the back of her tongue, as if his bad temper and short fuse manifested into an appropriate flavor. She turned, smiling up at Trapp.

"Is that because you didn't think I would be invited, or you didn't think I would come?"

". . . Both?" he winced, earning her laughter. "I'm very glad to see you, don't get me wrong. Look, I don't know what happened, and I really don't want to be involved, but I'm glad you're here. You're good for him. I hope he's good for you. I'm surprised, but it's a happy surprise."

"Well, this is the only Lupercalia shindig in town. I couldn't miss out."

He beamed with that megawatt smile, and she wondered, not for the first time, what he was doing, wasting his time with a human. "You made the right choice. This is probably your only chance to see me in formal wear. Get your last look, but it's about to be left in a heap somewhere."

Vanessa laughed. "Get to it then, brother wolf."

The ceremony was a near mirror of the one from antiquity. Sacrifice and thanks, sex and sweat. The wolves' eventual run was to take place counterclockwise around the hill upon which the Greenbridge Glen Estate sat, mimicking the run around the Lupercal, ending with the captured couples mating in an adrenaline-fueled frenzy. First, though, came the ritual.

Her inattention had caused her to be towards the back of the room once the ceremony finally got underway, and so she did not see the Luperci priests ascend the makeshift altar; did not see the anointing of blood and milk and oil, and only heard the echoes of the ceremonial laughter. Pomp and tradition, ageless and endless, a celebration of what they were and where they had come from. Grayson liked the pageantry of events like this, something older than any of them that still lived in their bones. He might be a self-centered prick most of the time, but when the opportunity arose for observance, he was as devout as a pack elder, turning his nose up to any half-hearted celebration, and she found she quite agreed with the sentiment. And since *his* nose was the only one that counted, the others did exactly what he wanted.

They gave thanks to the mother who nourished, paid homage to the first wolves who founded an empire and raised their voices to join in a ceremonial chant. The chase might be the fun part, but the ceremony was a crucial element in the evening's enjoyment, and if she focused hard enough, Vanessa was certain she could smell the olive blossom and honeyed wine carried on the air from that first, ancient ritual. Her eyes slipped shut, soaking it all in.

She was too far away to see the altar, but the distance had its benefits, for she was in a perfect position to observe the wolves as they entered. The headdresses completely concealed their identity but did little to hide their nakedness as they moved in a procession to the altar. The Brotherhood of the Wolf, a sacred sect born in antiquity, their practices still alive and well amongst modern werewolves, particularly in Cambric Creek. The men were short and tall, stocky and muscular, bare cocks in various stages of hardness and flaccidity, unidentifiable and anonymous. Her wolf squirmed, wondering how many of them would pursue her, whose lashes she would feel as they moved through the crowd.

Other Lupercalia celebrations used more pedestrian methods of choosing pairings — names placed in jars and pulled randomly, the paired-off couple disappearing for the rest of the evening, but such lukewarm arrangements had no place at these festivities.

Sex and sweat and screams were part and parcel of the ceremony, and they would not have it any other way. The celebration was primal in nature, the *true* old ways, as she'd learned over the last handful of years, when wolves were given the freedom to run and hunt, chasing their prey until submission, their coupling a prize to be won and not a game of chance for children. Any of these men might have her, and that was simply the nature of the evening.

That this year's ceremony took place so close to the full moon was happenstance, but a delicious one. The wolves would be heated and ready, their animalistic tendencies rising and their knots swelling every time their cocks grew hard, their breeding instincts triggered by the smell of women in heat. The seat-fillers would fill in the gaps adequately, and every wolf in attendance would get his dick wet by the end of the night, but there would only be a handful of others advertising their readiness. She wouldn't be the only one with a heat simmering shallowly beneath her skin, eager to be filled and fucked, but she knew from celebrations past that the numbers would be uneven, the she-wolves in shorter supply, making the ones who were there — like her — an even more desirable prize to be won. *And he does love to win.*

"What do we have to do?!" It was the human from earlier, the excitement over newly-acquired gossip washed away in a tide of panic, now that she realized there was more to the night than simply looking pretty.

Vanessa frowned. It wouldn't do to have the girl swept up in something she wasn't prepared for, not if she might claim she was forced later.

"You *do* understand what this night is about, right?" It wouldn't do to have complaints of dodgy consent, would reflect poorly on all of them. "If you don't want to participate, you should go upstairs now. You can hang back and watch with the other gawkers."

"No, I-I do! I know, I mean. The werewolves . . . I'm going to hook up with a werewolf. But what do I have to do?!"

She smiled at the girl, knowing her canines were longer this close to the turn.

"Well, you have to run. The chase is the fun part. If you don't run, you'll be taken as an easy prize."

"Is that bad?"

By then, the drums had given up any pretense of being anything other than a heartbeat for the crowd to churn against. Vanessa shrugged, gathering herself for what she knew was coming.

"I suppose not. Not if you don't care who catches you."

She heard the first partygoers cry out far behind them, the first slap of the leather against bare skin, and then they were off. The human girl squealed, making for the wall, and Vanessa bounced on her toes. She'd never been this far back in the crowd, and the rising tide of people cresting like a wave in her direction made her cry out in excitement, pivoting on the balls of her feet to dart out of the way. She serpentined along the side of the surge, waiting for the moment that the crowd split, and as soon as she saw her opening, she darted into the melee. *This* was where she was meant to be. In the midst of the running, whipping wolves, dodging the other partygoers as leather thongs struck the back of her thighs.

To her left, a woman screamed in laughter, shrieking shrilly when she was pulled from behind, an arm encircling her waist and lifting her off her feet. Vanessa dodged around bodies, determined not to be caught that easily. The wolves who claimed women in the ballroom were opportunists — positioning themselves strategically throughout the crowd, so they didn't need to compete to find their mate for the night. She supposed they were worried about a scarcity in prospects, as if there would ever be a shortage of women at any event he threw. She had no intention of being taken by that sort of hedge-betting strategist. She wanted to *run*, and any wolf that tried to claim her as the spoils of their victory would need to chase.

As she suspected, it did not take long for the well-heeled guests to lose a bit of their polished shine. She passed Tris Tatterswain near the base of the staircase, his arm around a braying woman with long, blonde hair and the neckline of her dress around her waist, her full breast cupped and overflowing from the palm of his hand. All through the crowd, clothing was shed and dropped; pulled away by the hands of staff hired to work the event, making way for the naked, wolf-headed men to weave through the throngs of people, wielding short lengths of leather, striking out at the women who deliberately got in their way.

***

The short one came after her first. The one from against the wall with the filthy mouth, catching sight of her as he careened through the crowd, swinging his leather thong back and cracking it against her thighs as she got hung up behind a petite goblin, one she recognized from the only adult entertainment shop in Cambric Creek, who was currently caught between whip-bearers who'd come up from the sides. His cock was short and thick like the rest of him, fully engorged and flush to his stomach, his foreskin already retracted to show a dark, hungry tip.

The foul-mouthed stranger was transparent in his desires and would no doubt be a satisfying prelude to the main course for the evening, and if this were any other night, any other celebration, she might enjoy bouncing astride his hips . . . but Vanessa knew her wolf would not be satisfied; knew the overwhelming need that rippled beneath her skin would not be quelled by him. Besides, she thought, skirting out of the way of a stumbling couple, he wanted to play the alpha with her, and while she clearly had a weakness for bossy, commanding men, her patience for taking orders was only so much, and that slot was currently filled.

Unlike some of the other guests, the stola she'd worn was designed for practicality, skimming above her knees and gathered at the shoulders, an athletic silhouette, perfect for running. She swung out of the way of the short man's whip, hopping on one foot and then the other, quickly relieving herself of her patent leather heels before darting back through the center of the press of bodies until she was confident she had lost him.

Bracing, midwinter air gusted in from the open doors at the back of the house, opening up to a wide veranda, steps leading down to an expansive lawn, and the ring of dark forest beyond. It was the forest she wanted. She wanted to run, *needed* to run, needed to let her wolf feel the wind in her hair, with nothing but the moon and sky overhead, outrunning all of her pursuers but the fastest, and she didn't want to do so on the pavement or across the lawn. There was no sport in that, no hunt, the chase a necessary part of the thrill of being captured.

The sharp bite of leather stung across the back of her thighs once more as a tall man approached her from the rear, swinging the whip back with fervor. Vanessa felt the crack against her skin a second time, then a third, nearly stumbling on the fourth, attempting to weave around the bodies surrounding her in an effort to get away. The man dodged, ducking back around the laughing couple who slowed her progress, managing to catch her once more. That he could have been anyone was the most exciting part, setting her heart hammering in her throat. The yacht club hottie, the handsome blonde with the pointed chin who'd been in the first conversation circle she'd abandoned . . . doctors, lawyers, bankers, company presidents — they were all here, rubbing elbows with art students and baristas, entry-level administrative assistants, part-time realtors . . . this wolf could have been any of the above.

He was tall, tall and somewhat broad-shouldered, and for the briefest moment, her blood thrilled as he caught her around the waist, thinking it was *him*. The scent of her captor caught her nose then — warm, golden-brown, dusty dirt roads and sun-dappled trees, and a watery cool, aquamarine-scented cologne that made her nose twitch, and she knew he was not the one, bore scant resemblance to the only wolf she hoped would chase her. He was not broad enough through the chest, his washboard abs too sculpted, his body honed for aesthetic instead of strength, and his smell was all wrong. His cock was hard, though, jutting out like a handle, and she gripped it as he swung her out of the crowd's path. Long with a steel-like firmness, he was longer than she was used to, and her cervix winced in her body. As her fist tightened around him, she decided he did not possess the girth she liked, the solid thickness that reliably made her scream in pleasure, and that if she were settling for a lesser wolf, she would have been better off with the stranger from the wall.

Vanessa twisted out of his arms, giving him a flashing smile of her own as he feinted, reaching for her again. Escaping his persistence was no easy feat, but she managed to find another break in the crowd, sprinting through bodies until the sharp night air sliced at her bare arms and legs. There was a sense of claustrophobia within the press of partygoers, people shrieking and laughing, jostling each other as they half ran, half-staggered along, and she increasingly felt as if she were being carried upon a fast-moving current rather than being fully in control, a sensation she could not abide. Leaning forward, she barreled through the bodies in front of her, cresting the wave until she was the lone leader, making for the doors.

She wondered, for the first time, as the open doors beckoned her forward, what would happen if Trapp were to be the one who caught her. The shock of the possibility made her slow for the space of several heartbeats, leaving her vulnerable to the wolves at her back, but for that brief moment, she didn't care. He was also tall and solid with muscle, athletic and fast, and he would undoubtedly be able to outrun most of the other wolves in attendance. His smell was one her nose knew, painfully similar to the wolf she wanted. In the heat of the moment, her nose might be tricked, the lust spurned on by the chase demanding to be satisfied, his similarity to Grayson in height and build and smell leaving her confused, and he might fuck her in the mud, right there on the edge of the treeline, and no one would ever need to know.

Nothing could be held against them on the night of the wolf, for the night was about the chase, and there were no repercussions for the couplings that might occur. Her mind conjured an image of his body curled over hers — solid and sculpted, hips pistoning, leaves in her hair, his cock hitting her in just the right spot, pushing his knot into her as he came . . . and then his smile.

His bright, mega-watt, panty-melting smile, the one that had the whole of Cambric Creek wrapped around his little finger, and her being forced to bear the brightness of that smile and the sparkle in his dark eyes, contemplating what they'd done until his knot subsided . . .

Vanessa cackled in laughter, shrieking when a leather thong caught the back of her thigh. It was the short stranger again, more determined to have her than she'd previously given him credit for. She continued to laugh as she threw herself forward, weaving through bodies until she was at the front of the press, bursting first out the veranda doors. *He would have the wolf head on, you wouldn't need to see him . . . but Trapp isn't going to catch you.* He would undoubtedly be a satisfying fuck, but the night would end eventually, and she'd be reminded that he was too bright and sunny for her liking, that he possessed a fiery temper instead icy aloofness, and that he wasn't the one she was running for.

Her toes curled over the edge of each concrete step as she hopped down, squealing when her toes hit the icy cold grass. It had been warm that week, an unusual spike in temperature for mid-February, but the forest would still be chilled in icy cold water, muddy from the melted snow. The thought did not slow her. *Run, rabbit, run.* She'd not been the only one to take to the outdoors. As soon as her feet hit the grass, Vanessa could hear the other revelers spilling out of the ballroom at her back, pausing in her retreat to eye the crowd.

It was then that she saw him.

She realized what a terrible choice she'd made in stopping, for the outdoor floodlights faced her, framing her in the spotlight for all the guests still on the veranda, leaving them in shadow for her. The short stranger from the wall had made it back to the front of the group pouring out of the doors, cracking his leather at the sight of her, stiff cock bobbing with his movements. He cackled when he caught sight of her, making for the stairs. To the far left, Vanessa thought she spotted washboard abs stumbling through the doorway, his arm draped over one of the seat-fillers, pausing when he saw her on the lawn, but neither of them held her attention as much as the man already coming down the steps.

The wolf in the center of the stone staircase walked with a confident, unhurried air, the same cocky swagger he had in the courtroom, his soft cock bouncing heavily against his thigh. He was a dark, hulking shadow outlined in the bright floodlights, moving with single-minded precision in a straight line towards her. Were she not the one in pursuit, Vanessa might have appreciated watching his form and the economy of his movements, for the instant his toes curled over the edge of the concrete where the icy grass started, he was lowering in a crouch, his long spine curling, prepared to spring forward in chase. The wolf headdress created a chilling effect as he gathered himself, and her blood thrilled. *Run, rabbit. Let's see how fast you can move.*

He was heavy and muscular, but she was light on her feet and nimble, and very, very fast. Vanessa threw herself into a run before his weight could carry him forward with any momentum. There were others on her trail by then, hers and other laughing, shrieking girls as well, leading a stream of pursuing wolves clambering down the steps, the stranger from the wall and washboard abs among them, none holding the advantage of the lone wolf in the lead.

The estate's expansive lawn streaked by in a black blur as she made for the trees, her feet tapping out a rhythm that ensured she didn't lose her footing on the wet grass, dodging around the trees and entering the forest as silently as she was able without sacrificing her speed. She heard a crash in the underbrush after only a few yards and hoped it was one of her shadowed pursuers, for if they were that loud and clumsy, she would have no problem outpacing and avoiding them.

The smell of the forest was pungent — black and wet, rising around her, and the wind cut through her stola as she ran. She could hear their loud and clumsy footsteps crashing through the brush, approaching from three different directions, with a growl at her back. Her pulse jumped in her throat, and she leaned into her run, picking up speed to increase the distance.

There were dangers in running this close to the turn. Spontaneous changes had been known to happen, bones shifting and cracking, lengthening beneath a moon this bright and large, snarling wolves all competing for the same thing. The memory of that night, the size of his wolf, the power in which he'd fucked her, his teeth at her throat . . . he was angry with her, but that would pass eventually. They couldn't turn the clock back on the things they'd done together, and she couldn't forget, as much as it would have been the easier way to end things.

The forest ringed the estate, and she'd be able to use the tree cover to make her complete circuit. The shallow, slow-running creek on the building's left side loomed ahead of her, her leap over it as graceful as a ballerina, landing on her toes, never slowing. Her wolf writhed beneath her skin, exultant under the nearly full moon, its bright light cutting through the bare tree branches.

She hadn't expected the man who came barreling through the trees, growling as if the change were already upon them, tackling her to the ground. She shrieked instinctively, cutting off on a strangled yelp, knowing the damage was done. The wolf was inebriated, and his hands were everywhere — sliding up her legs and groping across her thighs, attempting to push up her skirt. His breath was hot at her neck, the gnash of his teeth scant inches from her skin, and she realized how possible it was that there *would* be an accidental turn that night.

He had caught her . . . but barely. She had not come out tonight for *barely* and had no intention of being had by a drunkard. It was almost too easy to pull a leg under herself, using his shoulders for leverage as she pulled herself up and away from him, throwing him off easily. *Too late.* Her scream had been a mistake, and the others knew where she was now.

She could hear her three pursuers still crashing through the woods, one of them slowing already. The one to the right was heedless of the noise he made, too focused on charging after her . . . the short one, she thought. He had more stamina than she'd accounted for, and it would be hard to throw off his attentions for the night. Her heart was pounding, and she realized that Grayson might not be the one to catch her. There were too many at her back, too determined, too close. She could hear their hard breath, their low growls, the sound of their pursuit . . . but she could finish the run.

If she could complete the ancient circle, she could wait for them to come to her and take her pick. The treeline ended just a few yards ahead, the open expanse of lawn ahead, white and shining compared to the impenetrable blackness of the tree cover, and like a moth, she was drawn to its glow. Vanessa was confident she could cut through the clearing without issue, feeling the white light on her skin, her wolf rearing. It was the moonlight that was her undoing.

She broke from the tree cover, head dropping back and her arms opening as if to embrace the white beams of light, never seeing the dark shape of the wolf at her side until she was broadsided, a brick wall slamming into her with a force that made her see stars. The blow of his body left her breathless, wrapped in his heavy arms and rolled, protecting her from the impact of the ground until she was on her back beneath him, sandwiched between his thick thighs, the too-bright lights of the floods blinding her. She'd made it nearly all the way around.

The smell of him was as pungent and familiar in her nose as the pine and peat of the forest around them, and as his hand dragged down her throat, tightening at the base, her heart quivered, blood roiling beneath her skin. Helpless and captured. This *was* why she'd come, after all. Despite its softened state when they'd begun running, his cock was hard now, rising like a heavy club over her belly, his appetite for fucking whetted with the thrill of the chase.

Vanessa realized he'd likely been keeping pace with her the entire time, moving silently through the woods, parallel with her own route. It had been others pursuing her clumsily, and she could hear them crashing through the brush even now, now that she'd been caught. Her captor was unmoved by their approach, the blunt edge of his perfectly buffed nails still scraping over her throat slowly, and she was certain she could see his smug smile, even concealed behind the wolf head he wore.

"It looks like you didn't run fast enough, rabbit," he crooned, his rough baritone making her toes curl in anticipation of what would come next as his cock jumped against her skin. The stola was dragged over her head, leaving her bare, and one of her legs was pulled open, allowing him to settle with one leg in between her own, space to rub his cockhead against the lips of her sex, coating in her slickness.

She realized then just how close they were to the house, to the circular stone balcony, still filled with those who had not participated in the run, those guests whose staid cocktail attire had remained unmolested. They'd not run, she reminded herself, squinting in the blinding light, but they knew what the celebration was all about and had come to watch. *And now it's time to give them a show.*

She'd not yet answered him, and his thumb pressed slowly on her throat. It would take such little effort for him to block her airway completely, she thought, to choke the pissy, pouty look off her face for good, and she wondered if that was perhaps what she deserved. At least as much as he deserved every violent scenario her fevered mind had conjured over the years.

"Is this what you want, rabbit?"

His voice was a low scrape across her skin, and all she was able to do in response was whimper, desperate and writhing, keening when he pushed the head of his cock into her. He'd been absent from her bed for too long, absent from her daily life, and her body was greedy to welcome him home. Everything about him was solid and thick, from his broad chest to his tree trunk thighs, and it didn't matter how ready she was, how *needy* she was, how many times they'd danced this dance — her eyes rolled back as he pushed into her, spreading her wide and stretching her walls, her breath coming out in a wheeze until he was seated within her fully.

His pullback was slow and dragging, and when he thrust forward once more, she cried out. Over and over, a slow drawback and a forward thrust, burying himself balls-deep on every pass, and every time she gasped, whimpering as he dragged against her g-spot. It wasn't enough, for she needed him to rut her wildly, needed to be filled with his knot . . . but this slow, deep fucking was an excellent prelude.

It was then that she saw them. The spot in the lawn where he'd rolled her was straddling the edge of the illumination provided by the blindingly bright floods before them. The shadows of the black forest were at their backs, leaving them perfectly in the spotlight. He was still kneeling upright and had begun to pump into her steadily with the same hard, deep thrusts, his palm pressing down on her lower abdomen so that she felt the drag of him within her.

The position left her whole body exposed, glowing in the bright lights, and she saw the shape of the onlookers on the rounded stone balcony ringing the balustrade, watching her being fucked in the grass. Beneath the overhang, others had begun pairing off, those who had been caught up in the chase or those who hung back to watch, not wanting to run but still wanting to take part in the more carnal aspects of the evening, and she was able to hear them, panting and grunting, fucking in the dark.

They were not the only ones, she realized.

Grayson's knot had swelled, and she felt it pressing against her entrance every time his heavy balls slapped into her, his hips picking up speed, but over his shoulder, she was able to see who she thought was washboard abs, holding a moaning young woman over his arms, thrusting upwards into the girl. Another woman shrieked in laughter, spilling out of the treeline, the wolf who pursued her hooking her around the waist. They tumbled to the grass only a few feet away, wasting no time in their pleasure. Vanessa was able to smell the other woman's cunt as her legs were spread and the heat of the other wolf's sac as he mounted the girl without preamble.

The entire lawn had turned into a writhing mass of bodies, moans and gasps replacing the sounds of the drums. *This* was what the holiday was about. Turning her head, she picked out the heavy breathing of another wolf-headed man, slowly stroking himself, watching her.

"He's the one you talked to," Grayson murmured, deep and mocking, low enough for her ears only, "back inside. Did you like the way his cock felt, rabbit? Were you doing that just for me, or did you hope he would be the one to catch you tonight?"

She laughed, a short bark of a sound, scraping her nails down his solid chest, dragging through the dark hair there, and catching on his pebbled nipples. It didn't matter what he said, and it didn't matter what he'd done to hurt her, she decided, suddenly remembering the smell of another man's semen, dry and sticky on her breasts, and the look on his face as it caught his nose.

"His cock felt fine. Thick. It would probably be nice going in. But he wants to play alpha wolf, and I don't have patience for that shit. Did you like fucking that girl you took on my vacation?"

"Not really," he said bluntly. "She was a pillow princess, and I like someone who gives as good as she gets. I worked most of the time anyway."

"You didn't even remember the right place."

He pushed his fingers through her hair, his thumb brushing her chin.

"I remembered. I wasn't taking her to your shack on the water."

"Did she suck your cock better than me?"

At that, he laughed. "Rabbit, I think *I* could suck my cock better than you. What did he say to you?" He inclined his head towards the short one.

"He asked if I wanted his knot," she huffed, "and said he wanted me to choke on his cock." At that, the movement of his hips ceased, replaced by the shaking of his shoulders.

"Oh, if he only knew."

Vanessa cried out when he pulled up, her wolf growling and snapping furiously, having been denied what they both needed. "What are you doing?!"

"Do you want him to fuck you? See how good it feels going in?"

"No!"

"Are you sure, Nessa? Like you said, it's a wide-open field this year."

She scowled. "There's only one wolf I wanted."

"Well, nice to know. But it's good to remind them of the pissing order now and then, so I'm going to show him what you look like," he growled, pushing to his feet and lifting her by the arms until she knelt before him, "choking on a cock."

It was possibly the most humiliating thing he could have decided. Her tongue traveled the length of his thick shaft, pausing to lick and suck at the swollen base, letting her teeth drag over his knot until he growled . . . and then her mouth was filled, taking him in as deeply as she could as he pumped shallowly against her, pulling back after only a few seconds. Vanessa gasped as her deprived lungs sucked in the cold night air, drool connecting his cocktip to her lips, crying out in surprise when the leather thong he still wielded came down on her ass.

Once . . . twice . . . three more times. She sucked until she gagged on him, raking her nails down the front of his thighs every time he brought the leather down, choking as he reddened her ass.

He let her kiss down his shaft to the swollen base once more, and then her teeth weren't as gentle. His chest rumbled as her canines tested the firmness of his knot, her tongue moving over a swollen testicle, sucking it into her mouth as best she could, feeling the pulse of him. When her lips returned to his knot, she licked him, once . . . twice . . . three times, the same as he'd struck her, and her teeth sunk in, biting the meat of his knot until she tasted the copper of blood, her wolf howling.

She was on her back once more, fisting the grass as he mounted her, this time covering her body completely, exactly the way she liked, pinning her beneath his weight, filling her to the hilt on his first thrust. Vanessa cried out when he began to move, the slow tempo of earlier forgotten. Vanessa wrapped her arms around his wide back, her legs hitched over his hips, hooking her ankles to rest over the swell of his ass, and hoped the ground wouldn't decide to split open from the way he was fucking her into it.

"Who do you belong to, Vanessa?"

"You." She was gasping with every solid thump of his hips, breathless from the way he hammered into her, dragging against her, his cockhead kissing just the right spot. *Like puzzle pieces.* "I've always belonged to you."

"Are you sure, rabbit? I didn't think you belonged to anyone."

"I belong to you. Unless you don't want me anymore? Is that it, Gray? It's a piss poor way of breaking up, if that's the case."

The hand at the base of her throat tightened again, his thumb pushing into her mouth, and she bit that too.

"You belong to *me*."

The sound of voices rose, a moaning cacophony that filled the field — the sound of Lupercalia, and she eagerly added hers to the din, her wolf howling her ecstasy when her cunt clenched around him, his knot threatening to push its way in. She wasn't going to last long, not like this; not with the smell of and sounds of sex filling the air; not when he pounded into her without abandon, the solid, familiar weight of him above her like a comfortable anchor, too long absent. Her clit was being rubbed and rocked continuously from the way he kept himself angled against her, and she began to pant in time to his thrusts, higher and higher, the sound coming out of her more like a wheeze until the band of pressure snapped, and she ascended the wave. Her body clenched and shook, squeezing his cock as she screamed to the sky. Grayson growled, slowing slightly.

"That's it, babydoll. Hold me tight."

Her cunt was still quivering, but she clenched her muscles, all those Kegels coming in handy when she squeezed him again.

"Who does this cock belong to?"

"It belongs to you," he groaned; his knot finally popped into place, stretching her with a burn. She keened as his hips stuttered, filling her with pump after pump of his heat, filled with his cum until she bulged and her spine liquified beneath him, the lights before her blurring in a cascade of rainbow color as the world faded.

The time they were tied was her favorite thing in the world. Pressed to his chest, covered in his warmth and secure in his arms, she wanted to bite at his throat and kiss his wide mouth; wanted to press her forehead to his and breathe him in, every shift of their bodies a tugging reminder that they were irrevocably joined in this, that they belonged together, to each other.

It was then that he bit her. She was used to the feel of his teeth at her throat, grazing at her neck and nipping at her shoulders, but he'd never claimed her. It didn't have to mean anything, she reminded herself as his canines found purchase against the juncture between her neck and shoulder blade. It didn't have to mean anything because they weren't those kinds of wolves. They didn't live in packs; they weren't confined to the fringes of society. It didn't have to mean anything, but as a scream ripped from her throat as his teeth sunk into her, it meant everything. She wasn't the only woman he'd fucked, but she was the only one he tied, the only one he'd claimed.

"There," he murmured against her skin, his lips slick with her blood. "Just in case you forget again. Now they all know."

He shifted, simultaneously breaking her reverie and their tie, and she gasped at the unwanted separation, feeling both pitifully empty and pitiful for the sentiment. She was addicted to him; addicted to his knot and his smell and the way he fit inside her like he was meant to be there, hooked like a drug, and it would likely be her downfall.

She felt the gush of his release leaving her without his knot in place to stopper her once the swell receded, gasping when he pushed to his feet.

"I want you to clean her." His voice was sharp and dark, his courtroom bark, directed at the wolf from the wall, still only a few steps away. "With your tongue. You're *not* going to fuck her . . . but I want to hear her scream."

Her blood thrilled, and her wolf reared. She couldn't see his face, but she could feel his leer as the other werewolf nearly tripped over himself to settle between her legs, the hedonism of the holiday not over yet. The full moon was only a day away, and they would run again, she reminded herself, gasping as the other man's tongue slid over her clit, Grayson's cum still filling her. She would run, and he would chase, what they were built for.

***

In the end, it was Jackson who did her the biggest favor. Ironic, considering he was the sibling whose company she enjoyed least. She already knew the gossip, of course.

They'd relocated to one of the master bedrooms in the house, had showered and he'd fucked her again, hard and slow, had kissed her reverently, kissed the weeping red crescent of his teeth, kissed her chin and her nose and her lips, each eyelid, and for a time, the sound of his breath was the only thing in the world.

Now she rolled to her side, propping her head up to watch him as he sat on the edge of the giant bed, raking fingers through his dark hair, his back to her. Other men would have still been lounging against the pillow, snoring softly or working up the energy to rouse themselves, but not him. Once he'd slipped from her body, his mind would already be onto the next thing: the next case, the next trial, the next big thing.

Grayson pushed his feet and turned, finding and shaking out his shirt, slipping his arms through the sleeves before speaking.

"My brother is going to be mayor."

His voice held a note of uncharacteristic somberness, and Vanessa bit her lip, thinking of the endless gossip of the night. *Whispers don't matter, and you can't let them.*

"I think you mean he's *running* for mayor, don't you?" He looked askance in her direction as he re-fastened his shirt buttons, and she laughed. "I know, I know . . . how dare I insinuate that a Hemming not be given exactly what they want the moment they want it, presented on a silver platter to the adulation of all adoring onlookers."

"My brother is going to be mayor," he repeated again, a peevish note entering his voice, and that time, she'd sat up.

There was a tense set to his shoulders, a clench in his square jaw — tiny tics of aggravation and stress as she watched him pull his tailored pants back up over his hips. She sighed as his perfect ass was concealed, the tails of the expensive dress shirt smoothed beneath the waistband.

"You know, people can think what they want, but my dad avoided office so that we could have normal lives growing up, you know? So that we didn't have to grow up the way he did. But now . . ." The breath of frustration he'd blown out was another uncharacteristic tic, and when he'd sat heavily on the bed once more, Vanessa scrambled to her knees to wrap her arms around his neck. "Fucking Jackson."

"Okay, so Jackson is going to be mayor. What does that mean? What does that mean for you?"

He shrugged, "That's yet to be seen, but things are going to change. More scrutiny, definitely. No more of these parties, that's for sure. It's already started."

She wrinkled her nose at his words. "I don't think you need to do that. Everybody knows what you do, who you are. Everyone is already watching. Why does anything need to change?"

He turned to her with a scowl, rolling his eyes.

"Come on, Nessa, you know better than that. Once he's mayor, it's not going to be long until they're pestering me to take the bench. Time to step up. Keep my nose clean, do the whole model suburban family thing."

He'd pushed to his feet once more, and she watched him smoothing the crisp material of the shirt, adjusting his cuffs and collar until his reflection in the mirror had been returned to glossy, superficial perfection. Her stomach flipped and tightened, unsure of the insinuation behind his words.

"What the fuck is *that* supposed to mean?"

"Well, for starters, it means a sitting judge won't be able to fuck around with an associate from his old firm."

Her face had heated, fists balling in the sheets, the desire to throw something at him overwhelming.

"Wait, this is because I'm not a *partner*? I'm not going to be an associate forever, you asshole. What the fuck is this, a job interview?! The wound he'd left on her shoulder pulsed as her blood boiled. Fire flooded her veins, and then she *had* thrown something at him, but the pillow's strike had been less than satisfying.

It's not going to be long until they're pestering me to take the bench. His words jogged something, something that had annoyed her, just out of mind . . . A wheel began to turn, the pieces of a bigger puzzle slotting into place around the shape of them in the center.

"Why is Tris Tatterswain here?"

"What?" His voice held a note of aggravation, too distracted to process her question for a moment. "Tris Tatterswain has been on my father's payroll for years. He's harmless. He's a shitstarter and he knows everything about everyone, but he's harmless. For us."

Grayson does look so ***good*** *on camera.* Anything Jackson did, Grayson did bigger. It was his main ambition, his biggest weakness, his main point of malleability. Jack Hemming was setting his sons up like dominos, she thought, playing a very long game from his shining, golden tower on Main Street. *It's paving the road up for the next generation. If anyone actually thinks Jack has been resting on his laurels all these years, they've not been paying attention.*

"Well, I don't think you should take the bench. You're a trial lawyer. You love litigation."

"I will stop hating this job as soon as I can take something to trial. You know me far too well."

She smiled at his reflection, blood thrumming in her veins.

"Good, because you need to stay where you are for a while, get bigger experience, outside of civil work. Jackson is going to be stuck in place for what? Four years? Eight years? That's plenty of time for us to move you into something bigger. We just have to start working on your image. You need to start leaving your trial voice in the courtroom. No more making interns cry."

"I don't know *what* the fuck you're talking about. You're awfully interested in my five-year plan, rabbit. Planning on sticking around that long?"

"Are you planning on marrying me?" The words were out before she had a moment to review them; a sloppy brief he would have flung back at her under different circumstances.

He'd looked up, meeting her eye in the mirror with his quicksilver smile.

"You think you could hack that?"

She wasn't ready to stop running. She had no desire to tame her inner wolf, no matter how fucking stupid she was over him every single month, no desire to change anything at all, aside from the last few months. *Either a broken heart or a spring wedding, and both options sound ghastly*. There was only one path that led to keeping him though, and she'd rather follow it with him, and let a bit of her freedom go, than be lost without him again. The ladder, she thought, only went up.

"Are you insinuating I couldn't? Maybe I want to put the Hemming name back above the door at Dormir and

Shrike. You don't think I'm capable of playing nice and smiling for the local paper? You think this town is that fucking hard to maneuver? They think your mom is scary? Wait till they get a load of me."

He spun, his rolling laughter making her flush in a fury, until he'd leaned a knee on the bed, pushing into her space until he could press his lips to her forehead.

"Let's not go making plans to firebomb the community center just yet, rabbit. We can talk about tomorrow, tomorrow."

"Gray . . . "

"Tell me what you need, babydoll."

"Are you going to get tired of me if you're not chasing?"

His lips were gentle against hers, reminding her that she could've never conjured his kiss in her imagination.

"Maybe I'm tired of running, Vanessa. And you can try to run, rabbit, but it doesn't matter."

"It doesn't?"

"No, it doesn't." He gave her the sharpest smile he'd graced her with since the very first day he'd walked in late to her interview. "You belong to me. And I'd like to meet the wolf with the fucking audacity to try and take you from me."

"Good," she whispered as he looked himself over in the mirror a final time, leaving her naked on the bed. "And you're still taking me to Bora Bora, asshole."

Her eyes followed him as he left the room, the deep rumble of his laughter trailing in his wake. They weren't magically fixed, she knew, and they would need to have a long talk, an actual discussion about the future and they each fit into the other's lives and what would happen next . . . But tonight, he'd chased her, and she loved having Grayson Hemming chase her.

"Good," she repeated softly, falling back on the bed. "I have big plans for us."

* * *

Grayson & Vanessa will return in

Moon Blooded Breeding Clinic

MOON BLOODED BREEDING CLINIC

Coming Summer 2022

He smelled it the instant he stepped from the borrowed car.

Hot and swollen and dripping, the tumid, *delicious* smell of a heat. His mouth flooded, and the air in his lungs seemed to hitch, nearly rocking him off his feet. Lowell reached out for the hood of the car to steady himself as the world tipped, every drop of blood in his body racing away from his brain, being diverted to a far more pressing priority.

Closing his eyes, he forced himself to breathe. A long, slow inhalation through his mouth, sparing his nose . . . 2, 3 . . . then a hard exhalation, shaking his head, attempting to dislodge the lust-woven cobwebs. *It's fine, this is fine. She's probably on a suppressant. Focus on smelling the drug.* The smell of the heat suppressant was sharp and corrosive, like licking a battery, the opposite of alluring. Deciding his inner voice was right, Lowell sniffed the air, groaning as the smell assaulted him once more. A needy, desperate cunt, already dripping, begging to be filled, begging to be fucked, and he was equally desperate to oblige.

He wondered if Moriah knew how badly she was fucking with *his* biology at this point, and he *didn't* have the benefit of chalking it up to a head cold and a missed shot.

"I'm really sorry," she'd said mournfully, her voice through the phone thick with congestion and coming from a million miles away, or so it had seemed. "I didn't expect this cold to kick my ass. We'll have to wait until next month."

He'd brought her chicken soup and a small brick of compressed botanicals and bath salt, made by an Oni who'd hosted him earlier that year when he'd been on a shoot in Hokkaido. It was the surest way for her to gain some upper respiratory relief, and the soup was from the only delicatessen he trusted, run by a shifter family who'd moved to Cambric Creek from Long Island. He would take care of her while she was sick, and once she'd recovered, he would fuck her into the following month to make up for the lost time.

Visions of wrapping her in a quilt and feeding her soup were dashed when she'd opened the door a crack, peering out with bloodshot eyes.

"You shouldn't be here, Lowell. I don't want to get you sick! And I don't want you to see me like this. You're supposed to think I'm sexy, not a snot-covered mouth breather."

"We don't get sick the same way humans do," he'd called over his shoulder as he'd left her stoop, the door closing behind him, shutting him out.

Biologically inferior in every way. He could hear that particular, distasteful tone in his father's voice, the one that was specifically reserved for talking about humans, turning over and over in his mind, the thought making him slightly nauseous. What would he be contributing to this future child other than dark hair and height if everything exceptional he brought to the table would be stripped away, diminished and erased in a flood of chemicals?

Moriah was doing more than triggering her own heat with the shots — she was provoking his instinct to want to protect and provide, the thought of anyone even *speaking* to her while she was in heat making him snappish and short-tempered. He could think of nothing but seeking out the singular, mind-erasing hit of burying his cock in a needy, receptive mate at the height of the monthly frenzy . . . and now, *again*, she was taking it away.

And she wasn't, of course, his mate.

He had no intention of claiming or marking her, no plans to stick around Cambric Creek a heartbeat longer than necessary. He shouldn't care, and it shouldn't matter, and the fact that it *did* was the clearest sign of all that he was in too deep.

But at that particular moment, nothing mattered at all — nothing except the lack of blood flowing to his brain, making him dizzy, and the overwhelming smell of a needy cunt, making him hard. Lowell wasn't sure his brain was even functioning, synapses misfiring in every direction as he stumbled. He couldn't remember a time when he'd gone hard that fast, his erection scraping the inside of his jeans. His cock was calling the shots now, straining to see over his waistband, to be better able to direct his movements. His balls pulsed, the dictator in his pants demanding immediate action, a slaking of his lust, and he was helpless to do whatever his smaller head commanded.

If he closed his eyes and focused, he could hear her panting — high and rapid, a slight whine on every cant of her hips. He could taste on the air how wet she was, her desperation a sweet-metallic tang on the back of his tongue, and he wanted to coat his mouth in her slick before he gave her what they both desperately needed.

He had taken two steps away from the car when another smell caught his nose. Another wolf, another male, already there. A ripple of aggression moved up his back as he crouched, prepared to fight for the right to fuck whoever *she* was, to calm the fire under her blood, first with his cock, then with his knot; to fuck her until he went cross-eyed and emptied himself, allowing a trickle of blood to finally return to his brain.

He was halfway up the driveway when he passed the car. It was one he recognized.

Her name was Vanessa, and she had worked in the law firm where his brother was a partner, before Grayson had been pressured to leave corporate law for his current self-righteous pro bono gig. He hadn't been back long enough to ascertain exactly what sort of relationship his brother had with this woman, but Lowell knew she was his regular sexual partner, if nothing else; that it was *her* he smelled in the house and that Grayson was the other wolf he smelled.

Grayson, who had been born without a moral compass and had at least 60 pounds on him, most of it muscle. He wasn't sure what sort of neurological impulse it was that prevented him from charging into the house, cock in hand, but whatever it was, he was grateful.

His feet were frozen for several more heartbeats. He might win in a fight against Jackson, Lowell considered. His eldest brother was staid and professional; he spent his time in a lecture hall or chasing after his little boy, doing volunteer work around town, a perfect fucking Woodland scout. Lowell would almost certainly win in a fight against his twin. Owen hunched over a desk fifty hours a week, he and his girlfriend spending their weekends hiking and bicycling and otherwise being insufferably in love. Liam wasn't a consideration. Trapp and Grayson, however, were made of something different, something meaner and harder. He'd had his ass kicked by his two older brothers more times than cared to recount, and he knew that, despite what his drooling cockhead seemed to think, if he would ever challenge Grayson physically, he would likely have his ass handed back to him in a box, spare parts rolling around on the driveway.

His head was trying to turn him back in the direction of the pool house, his cock desperately trying to make him storm into the main house, but fortunately, wonder of wonders, the larger of the two heads prevailed. Not before he paused in front of Grayson's truck, flicking on one of the interior lights before slamming the door shut, making his way around the back of the house.

He had no doubt Grayson would be well-occupied for the next day and that he and his pseudo-girlfriend would not emerge from their bed until it was time to drive to the lake.

"You need to get laid," he'd told Lowell the previous week, making it sound like the easiest thing in the world, and Lowell supposed, for him, it was. Grayson was not helpless here, like a rat trapped in a rapidly shrinking cardboard box. This is where he'd chosen to stay, and he had a life here — a tawdry, gossip-spawning life filled with excess and probably too much cocaine, Lowell suspected, but a life nonetheless. Grayson had no conscience and was inured to the whispers around him, but Lowell wasn't his brother. He'd ignored Gray's advice, deliberately putting the orange juice carton back in the refrigerator with less than a swallow.

The full moon was in forty-eight hours. Two days in which to suffer through. He decided he would leave for the lake early; he would call Moriah to see if she was feeling better; to see if she was twisting in need, and remind her of what the following month would bring if she actually stayed on top of the fucking shots.

More importantly, he thought, holding his breath as he ducked around the side of the house — he didn't intend on still being there when Grayson finally emerged, bag packed, to find his car battery dead.

Read it NOW: https://linktr.ee/Monster_Bait

PRE-ORDER NOW - HOW TO MARRY A MARBLE MARQUIS

Dear Miss Eastwick, On account of the unfortunate incident involving Lord Pemberly and his valet at Lady Harthington's Ball, Her Majesty has no choice but to deem your Season a failure. With no other suitors of an appropriate station and no dowry, you are hereby ordered to attend the Monsters Ball, your last hope of securing a marriage.

Eleanor Eastwick is out of tricks. This alleged wallflower is hiding a secret, beyond the fact that her family is skint broke. If she wants to ensure the survival of her aged grandmother and younger siblings, she'll need to leverage the only thing they have left — their good name — and land herself a rich husband. There's only one problem she can see with her plan: she has no bloody idea what she's doing.

Enlisting the help of the wickedly rakish Marquis of Basingstone, Eleanor embarks on a crash course in how to attract the monstrous Gentry, high society courtship, and lessons in lovemaking . . . academically, of course. It never occurs to her that her tutor may, in fact, be a perfect match. By the time her heart begins to make her aware of its preference for the sharp-tongued, winged Marquis, the Monsters Ball is upon her and she needs to put her plan into action.

Lord Silas Stride, the Marquis of Basingstone, has no intention of giving away his heart. It would be cruel to chain another to the fate of a half-life such as his — only coming awake at twilight, living as a silent spectator to the daytime world. He'd not punish a wife in such a fashion; could not bear to allow his progeny to exist in a world where he resided only part of the time . . . far easier to embrace the life of a confirmed bachelor, and keep his heart as stony as the rest of him.

But Silas did not count on one Eleanor Eastwick. He recognized her the moment he saw her, seeking his disreputable counsel. She had shone like a star when he knew her years earlier, and she did once again in the darkness of his study, leaving him unable to deny his assistance. He could not possibly risk his heart on a delicate flower of the daytime, but a lady who was used to a life after dark . . . Silas Stride had no intention of taking a wife, but once Eleanor has left for the Monsters Ball, he cannot help but claim his own invitation, and his bride.

How To Marry A Marble Marquis is a standalone Regency Monster Romance featuring a Gargoyle/Human pairing that takes place in the shared universe of The Monsters Ball. It is the first book in C.M. Nascosta's Temptations & Tails: Monster Regency Romance series.

Pre-order now – https://linktr.ee/Monster_Bait

About Author

C.M. Nascosta is a USA TODAY bestselling author and professional procrastinator from Cleveland, Ohio. As a child, she thought that living on Lake Erie meant one was eerie by nature, and her corresponding love of all things strange and unusual started young. She's always preferred beasts to boys, the macabre to the milquetoast, the unknown darkness in the shadows to the Chad next door. She lives in a crumbling old Victorian with a scaredy-cat dachshund, where she writes non-traditional romances featuring beastly boys with equal parts heart and heat, and is waiting for the Hallmark

Channel to get with the program and start a paranormal lovers series.

Do you love exclusive short stories and character art? Join us on Patreon and participate in a vibrant Cambric Creek reader group, get exclusive access to work-in-progress stories, exclusive art, and much more!

https://www.patreon.com/Monster_Bait

FOLLOW C.M. NASCOSTA

Visit C.M. Nascosta's website for Content Warnings, blog posts, and newsletter signup: cmnascosta.com

Stay in touch on social media!

facebook.com/authorcmnascosta

twitter.com/cmnascosta

instagram.com/cmnascosta

Made in the USA
Middletown, DE
31 October 2024